DIES IRAE

by Ruby Spinell

THE PERMANENT PRESS
Sag Harbor, New York 11963

Library of Congress Number: 89-62926
International Standard Book Number: 0-877946–00-1

Manufactured in the United States of America

THE PERMANENT PRESS
Noyac Road
Sag Harbor, NY 11963

Chapter One

Anybody can see I'm not a writer. I'm into the simplicity of numbers. Unless words lend themselves to use by symbols representing certain values . . . I mean what use are they? My father, Eliaphus Daniel Janah, knew this. When he asked me to finish his story I figured he had ulterior motives. How much have you written, I asked. One line, he replied. Here is the line: The phone rang in the speakeasy of the Annunciation. What follows is the rendition of an accountant.

The phone rang in the speakeasy of the Monastery of the Annunciation, shattering the cloistral stillness. There was no one in the phone room to answer it. The buzzing chirping sound carried through the cavernous monastery building to the lay sisters kneading bread dough in the pantry off the refectory kitchen. They heard and ignored it. Two sisters in the chapel on solitary retreat, distracted by the continued ringing, tried in vain to shepherd their scattering thoughts. The young postulant cleaning the novitiate directly overhead felt a piercing sadness. While she lived in this house she would never again have a telephone call from her parents.

A door opened at the end of a long hall. The vsish-vsish of straw alpargatas padding broke the silence as a tall figure in a brown and grey habit and black veil came quickly along and thrust herself into the phone room, her heavy woolen scapular flying sail-like out behind her.

She grabbed the phone down from its cradle. "Deo gratias?" That inflective rise again. She heard herself and wondered if she were becoming a bit wary, praising the Lord with a question mark.

Commiseration deepened her voice as she spoke to the man on the line. The phone room, one of two, collectively called the speakeasy, was a barren room with no windows and two doors. A single forty-five watt bulb burned.

As she spoke on the phone, Sister Damian of Mary fiddled with the latch on the 'turn.' This curious contraption, intriguing first-time visitors to a cloistered monastery, was a large wooden barrel that had been sawed in half from top to bottom and set in the wall.

Hollow and revolving, this free-wheeling device allowed items to pass from hand to hand while the parties remained unseen. Visitors to the lobby of the monastery placed articles for the nuns on its shelves. The sister on 'turn' duty sent gifts to the laity.

Absentmindedly, Sister Damian swung the barrel left, then right; it was gliding easy again since they oiled the bearings. It must be about time for the mail delivery, she thought, I may as well leave it open. She swung it so the solid wall of the barrel faced her, the opening facing out into the lobby.

The front doorbell rang. She excused herself to the man on the phone and buzzed it open. Footsteps came right up to the wall.

"Deo gratias!" This time her tone was fervent and ringingly positive.

4

A muffled voice said, "Afternoon sister, these are for you. Poor you." He sounded like he had a cold. She waited, watching the drum make little balancing motions as he placed the packages.

"Take care of that cold!" There was no sound. She heard the front porch groan and realized he had gone, moving very quickly.

Poor man. What he needed was a cup of camomile tea. Trouble with these walls, you couldn't see when a simple charity was needed. You put out all the antennae you possessed, listened with your whole being, but you were never sure what was going on out there. At times she agreed that this was an outmoded aspect of cloister. She returned to Mr. Oliver holding patiently on the line.

"She's going to take the kids, Sister, I can't bear her taking the kids!" Sister Damian, picturing the quiet in that usually rambuctious house, winced at the lonesomeness. Murmuring something sympathetic, she swung the drum inward.

Usually there were a few packages, small gifts from the sisters' families, a smattering of letters, pleas for prayers, bills. So routine was it that her hand went instinctively to gather up the envelopes before taking the packages and placing them on the shelf to the side.

Something slid awkwardly as her fingers brushed it. Sister Damian stared in horror at the drum. On the upper shelf, three hands with very jagged wrist bones protruding had been placed wrist to wrist in a grisly star. The one she had touched slid forward on a slug track of fluid. The fingers curved upward, beckoning. She stepped quickly backwards. Her gaze lowered. On the bottom shelf stood three hacked off feet.

Their toes splayed out, perhaps caught in the act of grasping the ground from which they had been delivered. She stood mesmerized by one big toe that was three times the size of the others.

Senior Detective Eliaphus Daniel Janah sat in a divided room. One wall had been removed and replaced with a ponderous black grill. Fat black bars stationed six inches behind the grillwork reinforced its message.

He looked into the adjoining room, a very somber place with its black cross hanging on the wall and its uncompromising chair. Shaking his head in disbelief, he caught himself and sat upright, feeling for the moment as if he were being watched. Ahh, he'd seen too many peepholes in movies like "The Rose" and "Agnes of God."

An hour ago the lieutenant had given him this assignment. "It's your turf, Eli."

"I'm Jewish! Don't know a thing about cloistered monasteries except what I've seen in the movies."

"Well . . . Jewish . . . Catholic . . . same thing." Eli must have looked as disconcerted as he felt, for Morley pulled the cigar from his mouth and shrugged. "You know . . . come from the same seed 'n' all, don't they? Same stock. One's waiting. One said he came. Same thing."

So he had arrived, rung the front doorbell. Had the door buzzed open by phantom hands? He had spoken to the sister hidden somewhere behind the big wooden barrel. Asked for Sister Damian. Been instructed through another buzzered door. And here he was before this monstrosity of iron. What a place! Surely a different world!

6

There were muffled sounds, footsteps, and every now and then bells rang in different combinations. After the voice at the barrel said she would ring for Sister Damian, he counted six rings.

Coltish, he thought, as she came into the room. He winced at his assessment. How, Eli, can a cloistered nun be considered coltish? She looked directly into his eyes. He was six foot three. She maneuvered somehow between the bars and grillwork that were hampering him, and for a minute he caught a complete face, full coral lips, quizzical, grey eyes.

She thrust a hand through and gripped the crosspiece on the grillwork on his side in an unspoken gesture of reassurance. She sat very still, seeming to realize that he needed time to acclimatize. Then she introduced herself and asked him to sit down.

"How can I be of help, Detective? I've spoken with so many policemen already." Her voice was strong, yet quite soft.

"I understand, Sister, but I'm the one who has to find the bodies to go with the parts you had delivered." Her body gave a slight quiver. Great, Eli! Keep on.

She sat then in the chair and he immediately lost her eyes, disappearing behind a bar. Leaning over on one haunch to see if that would throw the face opposite him into some kind of whole, he realized suddenly how much he was accustomed to read from peoples's faces, that he depended on the features playing together.

He leaned forward and saw that the mouth opposite him was turned up at the corners. "You get used to it, Detective," she said, rearranging her chair. Now he had a clear view of the flicker in the grey eyes.

He should probably be grateful she had a face to show. Special permission had to be obtained from a superior to lift her veil.

"Please, Sister, if you would tell it to me as if you never told it before."

Looking steadily at him, she began.

"I was working in 'the breads,' they are the rooms where we bake, sort, and package altar breads, readying them for mailing to the parishes. I was called to the speakeasy by the phone." She laughed, and the flicker picked up a gleam of purple light. "That's the novices' name for the front turn. It wasn't a very eventful day." Eli wondered what might be eventful in a cloister. "At least until then. I wasn't expecting anything except the usual heartbreaks one hears at the turn." A fine wrinkle creased her brow. She did not seem at all harassed, but told her story calmly.

"The mail was due." She was looking down now at her cupped hands resting on her scapular. Mid-forties, Eli thought. Hands don't lie.

"You thought it was the usual mailman? Or was there an intimation it was someone else? Did you notice his walk?"

"My attention was divided, I don't know that I noticed his walk."

"But you knew it was a man?"

"Oh yes." There was no hesitation in her voice. "I knew as soon as he was against the wall that it was a man . . . a tall man."

"How tall is your usual mailman?"

"About five foot seven." She was silent, thinking of the consequences of that.

When she didn't continue, he spoke. "Before the individual

spoke, you knew it was a man and you knew it wasn't your usual mailman. Have you extra sense, Sister?" That may have been a bit wry, but he said it very gently. He was having trouble with bars and grills, and she could see through walls.

Two little spots of color appeared high on her cheekbones. "I don't have extra sense, Detective Janah. I'm a religious, not a psychic." He tried very hard not to smile and succeeded.

"You thought he had a cold? Would you explain that?"

"Well, it sounds ridiculous, Detective, but I thought he said, 'Poor you.' That wouldn't make any sense. His voice was muffled, the kind of stuffiness you hear from someone with a good head cold."

"He may have known you." Neither of them said anything further for a few minutes. There was a great calm about the woman, Eli thought, despite the pain lines in the face, maybe because of the pain.

She seemed to be lost in reverie. "I knew he had gone when I felt the emptiness and heard the board on the porch." She went on to talk about the loose board that the carpenter had checked and nailed down, the loose board that still squeaked, but Eli had the feeling her mind was somewhere else.

She repeated herself, "I knew he was gone when I heard that board and felt the emptiness on the other side of the wall."

"You don't have an extra sense, yet you feel through walls."

"Ah, Detective, that's different." She searched for a word and then abandoned it. "A human being generates a lot of energy." She smiled, causing the worry lines to join hands with the laugh lines and form a dimple on the right side of her face. The left side looked curiously sedate in contrast.

The wicked glitter of purple was back. "You, for one, have generated your own brand of electro-magnetic energy since arriving. Everyone does. You came right in up to the grill; many hang back. I knew you were male. I knew how tall you were."

Quite suddenly she looked embarrassed at the turn of her meanders. Briskly then, "I've worked the turn for many years, your senses become very keen, you must know this from your work." She swallowed her tongue on that, remembering how dumb she had felt talking to the empty hall. "It certainly isn't extra sense or any of that kind of foolishness."

Eli nodded agreement, and tucked away a reminder to pursue it again. "I'm very grateful for your patience, Sister. Would you kindly go through actually seeing the hands and feet for the first time? Any thoughts at all that come to mind." He tried to radiate calm electro-magnetic energy.

Sister Damian of Mary did not regain community immediately. When detective Janah left, she stood quietly in neutral country. She hoped Sister Alice, who was working the turn, did not get curious. Maybe she wasn't in the front of the house when he let himself out; there would be no question then about the closed door to the speak. Good-hearted. Always bustling, though. Oozing with sweetness and charity when one's need was for silence and quiet. How she could ooze thus without breaking into actual speech was beyond her, yet this was Sister Alice's specialty.

Sister Damian gave a deep, audible sigh and sat down in the black chair again. The floor was varnished to a high shine, with not a speck of dust on it. The three foot high black cross hanging on the wall held no figure of the crucified Christ; each novice was piously told to reflect on who now belonged there.

As a young woman seeking entry, she had been impressed

by three things at her first interview: the grill, the clean floor, and the starkness of the cross—the immutable sacrifice.

The sounds of Evening Prayer drifted through from the east wing, the nuns in chapel. Strange seepage. She remembered wondering how everyone knew what was going on in a house that did not talk but one hour of the day. Years in the cloister had taught her that an efficient network of sounds, silences, and intangible currents was constantly at work.

And so the unrest spread from the turn room today onward and upward until reaching the infirmary at the far western corner of the annex where old Sisters Philip and Barbara threw their water jugs in unison at good old gentle Sister Patrick, the infirmarian. Of course they knew not what they did; everyone knew they were quite senile. Even so.

It is difficult if not impossible to describe human remains in the sign language the sisters used to communicate the essentials. A lot of whispering ensued. From there it was a matter of degree. Heavy feet pounding. The running of the wire and phone jacks into the extern quarters. Click of cameras. The police initially whispered, but quite soon their voices rose to the level of men involved in their work.

The lovely sound of plainchant fell on her fevered brow. Then the chanting stopped. The lights were being turned off, the sisters filing out, youngest first. Off to the refectory for the evening meal.

The thought of food made her stomach lurch. Oh, they had scrubbed that wood. When the police finally left they bleached and SOS'd the shelves to a fine blond. In the enclosed space the fumes nearly knocked them off their feet.

The detective in charge . . . somewhat tightly held? Maybe

just the newness of the situation. He was Jewish; the eyes, the wavy hair gone to grey at the temples, definitely Jewish. But, of course, that would not be allowed to interfere with an investigation.

He carried himself easily; there was power there, but it was under control.

He dressed very well for a detective. Maybe they're changing too. All the books, well, she really hadn't read that many, but one hears this and that. Detectives are described as unkempt and slouchy, old food stains on ties, that sort of thing. She hadn't seen any stains, but some wear and tear, definitely wear and tear. He was very cool, very controlled with his questions. Professional, not overriding. I swear he was laughing, though. At least once, I know he was laughing and trying hard not to show it.

It was time to rejoin the community. Oh Mother, help! She uttered the words silently with all her strength, bowed her head and sat like that for a few more minutes. Then she rose and put out the light.

Chapter Two

Paws and boots but no pussy, woe is me." He hit a foot pedal under the table. A voice-activated microphone on a fine metal arm swung out from an overhead flood. The microphone, no bigger than a silver bullet, hit the bulbous nose. "Noses maybe, but no pussy." Eli smiled to himself. Manny's scatological turns of phrase occasionally made Eli blush, yet he was the gentlest guy. Eli trusted him with his youngest daughter.

The low whine again. The bullet whipped six inches, stopped, swung erratically, and finally hung stable. "Thought you worked homicide?" Manny Bozeman pursed orangutan lips and peered at him from under a single, untrimmed hedge of eyebrow. "Ain't none here."

Eliaphus Daniel Janah stood opposite the parade of single file hands and feet. His gaze on one foot, he was thinking of *National Geographic* photos of ears, pointed heads, long lips.

He gestured with his head at the foot, "A new feat in accentuating a foot."

Manny shot him a look of disbelief. "You know they don't belong together." This was neither question nor declarative statement.

Emmanuel (Manny) Bozeman put out his hand and pointed

13

with his finger like a prissy teacher, gesturing to the hand at the head of the class, "That is a woman's . . . fortyish . . . maybe forty-five. Every one here, except one," the orangutan pursed, "is at least forty. Two are close to eighty. Two have been pickled; they've been sitting in Formalin for over a year. Two have been frozen. Two are fresh." He wrinkled his nose. "Well . . . not so all-fired fresh they don't stink. They've been refrigerated for about seven weeks. Two women, four men . . . I'll have it written up nice and neat. In fact, if Sue's here," he hesitated, "I'll have it in your box in an hour. By the way, all were taken alive."

Deciding not to wait, Eli took Route 100 North. Where it curved, bypassing Valhalla, he braked inadvertently. At least I no longer flick the right directional, ruefully at that . . . ahh. He drove the Nissan Sentra in at the first gate of the community college and through the middle of two almost empty parking lots, heading for the fuller one close to the library building. He eased between a seventy-nine Dodge truck with a license reading I GLIP and a new Ford pickup with a full gun rack. The working class had all gone back to school.

When he asked the young librarian where he would find information on the Congregation of Prompt Succor, he thought her eyes resembled the scene in 2001 where the embryo is being shot through vast reaches of empty cosmos. He did not know what women did to their hair anymore. The unkempt look, the rattier the better. No soft waves or curls, nothing to stroke. Everything frazzled and uncombed. Like Mir's when she got up in the morning, when she was absorbed in a piece. Hair that signaled, 'Do not pet the lion.'

"It's a religious community, a Catholic religious community," said the young woman as she directed him to the second floor stacks.

He found six books by Thomas Merton; two he'd read as a young man. Now there was a regular guy; you could talk with him if you met. Fat chance of that, though, him being cloistered and dead. His fingers wandered along the spines of the books. How did Prompt Succor differ from the Trappists Merton belonged to or the Franciscan Poor Clares or, his hand stopped on the *Book of the Foundations* by St. Teresa of Avila, translated by one E. Allison Peers?

Encouraged by the quiet—not at all like the college his youngest attended, where the entire student body went to survey the territory or be picked up—he pulled three volumes from the shelf, went over to a soft corner chair, and sat down.

Less than twenty minutes away by car, a woman was striding, smelling the dirty-sock scent of autumn on her three acres. She tried to scatter the leaves off to either side as she walked, but they had matted into the u-shape of the paths, decomposing into a slick that only a determined rake could dislodge. Not feeling like turning back to the shed for the rake, she picked her way, finding a tuft of grass here and there for her Nikes. She noticed at fifty that if she strode as always, she occasionally landed on her bottom. And so one tried for circumspection, for the sake of oneself, of course.

Mirari Buttrick Janah's parents named her Mirari—to be surprised at. As she learned a little Latin she realized how lucky she was. It could have been disastrous. Her father with his penchant for the classics could have named her after his favorite sheepskin, "Pellis Ovilla." Or after the Muse of Poetry

15

and Dance—Terpsichore. At fourteen, when she found him eating a plate of oysters with great gusto, she sighed and thanked God. It could have been Ostra. Brrr.

Whatever was going on when her sister was born resulted in the name Denique—finally, at last; Denique always claimed she was the Frenchie one. Five years elapsed, and one day her mother came home from hospital with: Quin—why not? Life! so many pressures lift with the emptying.

Her father had almost been a priest. But then, of course, if he had been a priest she wouldn't be here. He was twenty-six, finished with the Diaconate and ready to go into private retreat before ordination, when his mother became seriously ill. In those days the gates did not swing easy. But he received the necessary permission to visit her in the hospital, and there he encountered the nurse's aide.

For Mir, now, it had been three years since she had walked these paths, three years since her breakup with Eli. It took that long to heal, took that long to realize she wanted to live in her own house. The very instant she knew this she called the real estate agent and pulled the rental off the market.

She was fairly tall, about five eight. Against the autumn cold she wore a threadbare hooded sweatshirt in two kinds of green material; the sleeves had shrunk and been extended with the fluffy stuff of a toddler's sleeper. She had a square chin in a long face and blue-green, sometimes grey, eyes with heavy lids. A man sidling up in a diner once told her she had the softest eyes he had ever seen. Another time, from another man, she heard about a plastic surgeon who could take care of her problem.

Mir was fifty that year, but she always said she was fifty-three or four or five. Fifty seemed too young to her. She felt

16

too good to be only fifty. She had married twice, had given birth to five children in various states of incomprehensible anguish, euphoria, excitement, and despair. All were presently, for the most part, healthy young adults going blessedly on their individual ways. Her former husband said she was hurrying to her death by claiming years she did not have. Swept along, she felt was more like it. In these times to stand in one place seemed like hurrying.

The denim about her calves and thighs was full of snags from briars and cats. In long, slow strides she walked down the hill to the house. If she halted and gazed west at this point her eyes would dart, swallow-like, over all the houses and most of the trees. In 1910, the builders of the huge modified gambrel had built far from civilization. Even today, the land dropped abruptly and the swallow skimming her roof would not see another house through a vast ocean of leaves.

The schist to the south of the house sparkled in the angled sun, flat as a table, so good for driving small, three-wheeled cars, bottom-loaders, dumpsters. Just to see it triggered mechanical memory, the kind activated by alliances that rub.

A second type, logical memory, was fading with age. It was this that she had used when her son Pete was in his troublesome teens, memorizing names and phone numbers of all his (loosely called) friends, in case she had to trace him.

A third type, heart memory, occupied the place of honor now. Simply put, the more deeply moving the event, the more gratitude it brings back. As she gazed at the flaggies, she realized that far from triggering mere mechanical memory, the flaggies were definitely heart.

A wine-colored cat and the muse went out . . . The poem stopped abruptly. Two cats moved into her peripheral vision, gauging how sedentary she was going to be. A blue fire started in the apple. The cobalt dragon hissed a stream of saliva and steam drooling from its mouth. Metallic blue winking, triangular shield-like spines sprang up along the top of the dragon. The memory that makes it with you, my friend, is outside time and place.

The older cat jumped easily onto Mir's thighs and settled there. The younger, after standing on tiptoe, hooked her claws, pulled, but could not quite make it, her stubby legs flailing the air. Mirari caught her bottom in her palm, and lifted.

The heat from the fire grew. She thought of her article on Paul Valery; she had two weeks to draw it together. Valery has Socrates in the Architect talk about the infinity of act. He reserved for this transcendence every bit of energy not actually necessary for everyday living. She put the cats down on the carpet.

She slipped out of her jeans and underpants, as an afterthought taking off her shirt. Leaning back she opened long legs to the heat.

Attention is very important. Apple gives a lovely flame. Shifting to low sucking sounds the dragon dared to be dipped, dared to be spread over thighs, swirled around a smooth belly. A beaded blue dragon steamy in its center dropped heavy on her breasts. The aureola metamorphosed. Silky fine cheek of newborn suddenly reacted. Tumult, upheaval. Prehistoric nipple, becoming intact darkened plug from which years of sediment had washed, stood sentinel.

She lay in her own liquid, her own light. A wind moaned at the entrance to the chimney. The dragon whipped a jagged tail. Yes. You I do as if you were a stranger, her hand slid over the wet. In the eyes of the mob there is no carpet on which to throw the cats when the god arrives.

She woke on the floor wrapped in the queen-size down coverlet, breathing ash. One arm wooden. A small bundle of fur fell off her back as she eased herself up. Clam, watching Chowder bury turds in the cooled hearth, dislodged from her perch, made herself comfortable on the pillow. A downdraft sent another cloud of ash her way, she coughed, decided it was cold, lay back all in one motion.

She lay on her back feeling the steady ground; there was no rumbling beneath her, no tremors through the silent timbers of the house. It was quiet. No background roar of traffic punctuated by horns despite the fifty-dollar fine. No sirens.

A jet leaving a long, straight, white tail flew into the face of the wind. The tail became a squiggly line, then broke into Morse code. By the time it reached the far window, its passage was erased.

Coffee! She stumbled over the comforter, caught herself, headed for the kitchen followed by the two cats who saw action with possible food consequences. Scrabbling about in boxes is not what I like to do first thing in the morning . . . then you should have established some order last night. The dialogue ended with a smile of triumph as she pulled a sack of fresh grind with the Cheese Emporium logo in pink and black from the bottom of a box of dried cereals, nuts, and grains. Everything was going to be all right.

Soon the perc of the hot bean warmed her enough to discard the bulky garment she was dragging about while feeding the cats. Then, picking it back up and wrapping it about her, she settled in a rocker and drank the first of eight cups of coffee black.

She'd never done an article on Valery. Too close? Like writing of a lover and a friend? He hadn't been college fare when she went to school. Over the years when his name was mentioned, more often than not she noticed a blank stare or vehement emotion, usually negative.

He had strange grey matter. He was a hybrid much like Monsieur Teste, all idea, no act. They abhorred him, thought him precious. Yes, precious. "The life of the intellect is an imcomparable lyric universe."

A woman drowning in snowsuits and rubber boots, school schedules and broken toys read it, squared her shoulders and breathed deeply. Running babysitters back and forth, she thought Valery. Substitute teaching, she read Valery. Nursing a child, she held the child and Valery, pitting her intellect against everything of his she could find to read. Without this she would have died.

And when the self started falling back away from the newly emergent she was not fearful. Having read of his own intellectual crisis, her subsequent choice of conscious over secondary self was supported. Woman needs like minds when the choices she must make are so utterly frowned on by society. How much she owed him for the pure and absolute form of his work!

At the Monastery of the Annunciation, morning work was not going smoothly. The three women in the low, white room under the naked light bulb glanced toward Sister Damian, her press making great gurgling sounds, the metal trough-collar filling. Multiple white rapids shot over the edge while she lunged for a dish towel with which to cut off and dam up the flood racing toward Sister Anne across the counter top.

She could feel the reproof in the brown eyes. Nothing would be said that evening, no good-natured joke made in reference as would have been the way when they were in the novitiate together. The drawn lines were getting too intense, the increasing factionalism leaving little room for humor. With a wry sense of shame, she thought, how divided a house of prayer can become!

But the splitting of the community into enemy camps is one thing, she lectured herself, your mind-wander since yesterday is something else! Twenty-three years in religion and you call this custody of thought? She was a reproof, a humbling to herself, and feeling so incredibly jumpy. At least six cups of seared batter hung in loops and onion rings on the baker.

She shot a look of apology toward Anne, but the smaller nun was bent devoutly, her hands making little patting gestures along the edges of two stacks of pure, white unleavened sheets reading them for the cutting after Vespers. Since the violence of the world had turned up under her nose yesterday Damien could not shake the nagger.

Can you bring this sort of thing down on yourself? Yes! the nagger answered, shaking a bony finger like a metronome, 'and the inner shall be outer and outer shall be inner . . . You attract what you deserve.'

When the wooden clapper sounded its nada nada nada to end morning work period, all twelve-inch diameters of stainless steel shone, but she had not begun to chip the dough hardened on the back hinges. And the feet which held the heavy apparatus with its domed lid eight inches off the counter wore cotton between the toes.

She'd speak to Reverend Mother for more time to clean up. Putting six good sheets above her on the shelf and covering them with a clean cloth, she threw the yellowed ones under the counter in the discard bin. Burned. As burned as any first year novice called down for her pride to do penance before the refectory cross.

Who wants to be handed the burned body of the Lord at the altar? Now, if they were still laying the host down where they used to you might hang it on bad breath.

She thought of Johnny Nelson. He was such a devil. His mother, somehow perceiving this, brought him routinely to Mass hopeful that the atmosphere was catching. She pictured him getting his in his own grubby paw. Squinting, then holding it up, 'Hey Father, mine's burned!"

"That order has to be out by three. How much more time do you think you'll need?" Reverend Mother Michaels, looking diminutive in a Sears white nylon blouse sprinkled with blue forget-me-nots, had great black circles under her eyes.

"Are you all right?"

"I should be asking you that."

"I'm sure I can finish by Vespers if I go directly from noon meal." Sister Damian tried to breathe confidence.

Mother Michaels thought the tall woman in the long, heavy, wool habit was doing very well, considering. She herself hadn't slept at all last night.

Only the senior sisters had been given the stark details. But, of course, everyone knew something was not right. The tension in the house was too thick to wish away or disguise.

Damian was far and away the most extraordinary woman. Thank God, it had been she on the turn. A chill went through Michaels; remembering froze her whole body, and she wished she was wearing the old, heavy wool again.

To think that what they wore had been an actual matter of concern a few days ago. When she initiated changes, she expected that some of the older nuns would not take well to drip dry. She had given quite a few talks on poverty, stressing the cost of woolens. After all, they were not yuppies, and she preferred something simple that could be purchased by mail.

Half the sisters were now wearing something from the Sears catalog. They had even asked permission to purchase a perm kit. Looking over the community from her vantage point at the back of the chapel, she saw an assortment of stripes, flowered blouses, and skirts as well as floor-length habits.

Clothes seemed so inconsequential now. The person or persons who did this thing could not be in their right mind. She felt extremely threatened. The police assured her the sisters were not at risk, but how could they be sure?

Why had they been chosen for this singular gift? She had issued very strict orders about the use of the grounds. All outgoing letters were to cease for Advent. She had to tell the community, and being unable to write home about it would cut down talk. It was her responsibility to protect the nuns, and she had never felt more inadequate.

Their life was so much more than what they wore on their poor bodies. But there was no doubt about it, she looked at Sister Damian standing before her, the habits were beautiful.

"Sister, when are you due to go back outside?" Clothes might be individualized, constitutions interpreted more in the light of the times, but no one argued against active work in the world one year out of every four. Three years within cloister. One year outside. Their foundress had been very wise.

"Twelve months. Mother."

"Thank God you're here now!"

"We're going to weather this!" Sister Damian heard her voice; it sounded much more confident than she felt.

"Your cuffs are pretty worn, Sister." Michaels gestured to Sister Damian's sleeves. Women talk about inconsequentials when something too big for words rides heavy on their hearts.

"Take whatever time you need for the order. I think the chapel in the new development is pulling quite a following."

Chapter Three

Luciano Pavarotti sat in an empty concert hall, arms outstretched, index fingers touching the poles. Eli put fresh
masking tape under the sagging corner of the poster, rubbing
a sweatered arm to secure it. Never, never tape! If you can't
frame, pin. He heard and did not care; he and Luciano were
not for posterity.

He sat back down in the breakfast nook, lifting the luke-
warm coffee. Pavarotti reminded him of a modern day Buddha,
feet up, arms out, bottom down, stretched nonetheless, trying
to contain it. Trying to hear it first, then contain it. Like one
of those rotund Eastern hermits of Mir's wandering their cloud
scrolls, eternally hiking the Karst mountains of Guillin. He
would like to visit those rounded bolder mountains of China.
No one outside China believed at first that they actually ex-
isted: they thought them poetic license.

He glanced around at the neatness of the tiny kitchen.
Someone had been quite bold to run pipe up the turret of the
old three story Victorian, placing the kitchens in triple rounds
of light. The neighbor below, a woman in her thirties, grew
a profusion of plants. He had glimpsed the lush green when,

her door open, a slightly plump blonde dipped turds from a pan into a coffee tin and added fresh litter from a sack in the hall closet. She was often engaged in this activity when he came home from work, no matter what the hour. She was always pleasant, but he passed on, climbing up to his own landing, feeling courtly and ready to retire.

He'd never found the casual look. One of his daughters called him the dapper detective. Sounded like something out of a murder novel. Well, dapper hadn't spirit according to Mir, dapper wasn't spontaneous. Was it dapper that got you in a three-room apartment by yourself at a time when you looked for a mellow wife in your life? No one answered.

Not bad, though, he thought. Sitting up 'til all hours reading about contemplatives and contemplation made a man reflective.

As he stretched his long legs to the cushion of the opposite chair, the phone rang. Putting his feet back under him, he rose upright in one easy movement without touching the table. When I have to pull myself up, then I retire!

"Dad, great day huh?" The voice did not need an introduction. It didn't wait. "Awesome!" It was always difficult to pinpoint what his son was referring to as currently awesome. "Did you know Mom moved back into the house?" And the whirlwind came out of the north and their work was as a wheel in the midst of a wheel. Like a pop-up toaster, his memory brought the warm beginnings of Ezekiel; had Zeke or Mir nudged it?

"No, I didn't know. Did you talk?"

"I tried to call but the phone isn't connected."

Eli thought of Mir's periodic drifts into spirit stuff, times when she would not or could not pay attention to the details that held the body stuff together. How angry he would get! And now, he wondered if she had filled the oil tank; did she have food in the house? Did she make plans or did she just land back in their old home?

"How did you know?"

"Rosie's best friend works at Kippingwood."

The young lady's name was new; he deliberately did not refer to it. She was probably one of the family, as indeed his son told him they all were, all the young ladies. As heartwarming as this might seem, this extended family em—barrassed him. Occasionally, over the years he had given man-to-man monologues on sexual intimacy, AIDS, and her—pes while his sons smiled indulgently.

"Did your mother quit her job?" He silenced a little ripple of guilt at thus pumping a son about his mother, for, of course, Zeke had been the one to call.

"No, she's keeping three days of proof-reading and taken on more freelance. Guess she wants to write more and wants to be out of the city to do it. She took the house off rentals. Is going to ride the Central Monday, Tuesday, and Wednesday. What have you heard from Becca, the Bean Counter?"

Eli shook his head at Zeke's slaughter of his sister's lovely name. "Rebecca is doing just fine. She left a numbers theory book here before dashing off to Boston for a conference. She's thinking of going back to school."

"Decided she doesn't want to be a numbers cruncher . . . awesome!" Eli held his tongue.

A dark grey was building up to the north, the wind illus—trating again where he needed to apply fresh glazing com—pound to the windows. He always felt more harried when the earth darkened.

Zeke was still talking. "How about supper one of these nights?"

"Yes, de . . ." Eli made his response quick from long experience, but 'finitely' was spoken to a hum. He smiled to himself. Yes! Awesome.

The phone, laid back down, immediately rang again. Without altering the position of his feet, knees bent, back straight, he picked it up.

"Eli? Manny here." Bozeman was as succinct as usual. "Two Eurasian, Eli. Four Asiatic. Gotta go." Again the hum. Not American, not Indoeuropean, but Asiatic. How could he be sure? Was he ever wrong? As precise a man as Emmanuel Bozeman?

From the Chuckchi Peninsula almost touching Alaska . . . down under through Japan to the Sundas above Australia . . . north and east through Arabia and Turkey . . . north again along the Urals . . . all of this was, if he remembered correctly, Asia. One does not search an area that large for individuals with missing appendages. If only they had come from Westchester, New York.

Shifting weight onto one foot, knees bent, he flipped the Rolodex, then poked several buttons.

"Marion? Eli Janah. I'd appreciate time to talk with you. I don't know yet, but I might be dealing with some kind of ritualistic occult." His voice became apologetic, "I know they encouraged attendance, but both dates came at crucial times. I couldn't leave. I'm certainly no authority on cults. Please?" He could be very persuasive; it made no difference, men or women. They made a firm date for the following Friday to discuss the normal nut and the satanic crazy over lunch.

A minute and a half is a longtime to hold a phone listening

to it ring. The voice that answered was not Sister Damian's. It high trebled along in some alpine meadow sticky on the felsenmeer. The brittle cool kept the honey crystallized, it did not drip or run.

"I'll have to ask Reverend Mother, Detective. We're very busy here today. Will you hold?" Silence. No muzak. No classical Liszt like he had piped to him from Roosevelt the day Mother died. "Detective Janah?" Little crystals of honey broke off, "Mother says you may speak with Sister Damian at three." He thanked the voice and put the phone down.

Increasingly, dark clouds hurried overhead as he drove, the grey settling heavy around the car until, meeting up with Bert Hamill Parkway—tortuous as it was—he shot off on what he knew to be a quicker route, snow imminent.

A dark cross against a glowering wash came in view briefly as he swung off at exit nine. It reappeared, reigning high above a triple tier of rambling red brick. Each window in the building had been frosted at least half of the way up. Around this Edwardian castle, completely obscuring the first floor, was a ten-foot black fence extending to the right as far as he could see. Evidently, it enclosed a substantial piece of grounds, and to the left it ran on until it fitted snugly against the main entrance.

This approach from the rear gave one an impressive view of the wall. Yet, all walls can be scaled. He took in the residential nature of the ranch style houses; and the monastery's enclosed garden. The developer had placed the streets like the spokes of a wheel, and Eli wondered if the monastery was indeed the hub of a not seedy, but definitely lower middle-class community.

29

A stretch limo angled over to the few parking spaces before the chapel, so he continued on, finally finding a place on the street.

Three figures in clerical black were descending the steps as he approached. The beefy older man in the center looked up briefly, sizing him up, and then resumed talking, making very emphatic gestures with broad pink hands. The men on either side, one a middle-aged man with a pronounced stoop, the other a thin young man in glasses, never looked up.

"We can give you a lift, Father." The limo driver opened the door. "It's not far, Your Reverence, I'll walk." The broad-shouldered cleric shrugged and climbed inside, the younger man with the glasses following. A powerful engine purred.

Now, the eyes were on him, from the privacy of the dark, tinted glass: his age, size, condition, the slightly worn pinstripe with the matching vest, down to the new shine he'd given his shoes, all catalogued.

"Do you consider what has happened a sacrilege?" Eli asked.

There were dark circles under Sister Damian's eyes. She spoke very softly at first. "Elegi et sanctificavi locum istum, ut sit." Then her voice gained strength. "Ibi nomen meum, et permaneant oculi mei, et cor meum ibi cunctis diebus." She translated for him, "For I have chosen and I have sanctified this place, that my name may be there forever, and my eyes and my heart may remain there perpetually."

He had known as soon as she reached 'sanctified,' "Second Chronicles, chapter seven, verse sixteen."

"You know your Old Testament, Detective Janah."

"I'm not that familiar with the Latin."

"Well, when you recite the Divine Office every day it will

become a second tongue." Again, there was that glint in her eyes.

"It is an astute question," said the nun. "His Reverence Bishop Danley just left. We had a purification and reconsecration ceremony." She gave a little laugh, "I think it was mainly for the laity. Visitors to the chapel, and of course the turn, have increased tremendously, everyone peering for blood stains. The local paper did not play the morbid aspects up, but they did not exactly leave them out either. Sensationalism, news . . . you know . . . always wins in the end. Donations are up." Eli could feel her weariness through the intervening metal.

"Sister," he repeated, "do you feel this was a sacrilegious gesture?"

There was a long silence. "I feel it was a trust."

Poseidon farting fathoms under water . . . a low rumbling broke the silence. His stomach growling, he shifted his lanky frame quickly, pretending he was searching for a handkerchief. He had not eaten.

Sister Damian, rising as if she had left a faucet running in a stopped-up sink, excused herself, "I will quickly return." She left him and the old fart rolling boulders about the deep of the barren rooms. They weren't even warm, he thought. Wonder what kind of heating arrangement is installed in a big old place like this, must be drafty as hell. He never thought of hell alongside heat. It was cold; biting, congealing, bitter cold.

Heavy snowflakes whirled behind the clear upper panes of the windows as if caught in conflict. Between the building and the cloister fence they rose and fell like Kaballah angels ministering to the Sephiroth up and down the line of worlds. Those ascending rose more forcefully. He was intrigued by this.

"There is a good probability Eliaphus, you have the mind," and at this point he would emphasize by pounding his heart; the little red shawl tassels leapt. "You have the heart. Your father tells you this in all seriousness." Papa. Ahh. What do you think now? Talmud. Kaballah. Law. Criminal Justice. Where was the thread? A rabbi . . . it would have pleased you.

The door from the cloister into the speak swung inward, an uncontrolled arc hitting the wall. Sister Damian backed in, arms encircling a huge, oval tray, veils and habit all lop and flurry of heavy wool. She swept the tray onto a round, black table, then leaning forward to the bars, bent low and pulled the handle on a deep wooden drawer. some dark brown strands streaked with grey had escaped the white band across her forehead; they clung damply to the flushed porcelain of her forehead above little beads of perspiration. All was motion as she turned repeatedly, emptying the contents of the tray into the drawer.

"Now Detective Janah, if you'll kindly open that card table standing in the corner by the window, open it by your chair, you can lay these few things out. I don't know where my mind was."

The rich, hot smell of fresh coffee filled the barren speak-room. Eli picked up the hot coffee pot with the pads provided, leaving one pad underneath when he placed it on the table. He put a lovely, thick, white pitcher of cream beside a large, white mug. Bent again to a great platter of sandwiches: inch-thick homemade bread, chicken, lettuce, and cheese.

He couldn't remember later if he demurred before this largesse. It wouldn't be like him, he loved food too much. He did persuade her to have a cup of coffee with him. He could not with any equanimity sit there eating while she simply watched. The sandwiches were not the size you might envision females biting into; they were huge. He could find no fault with that at the moment and wondered where she learned to make decent sandwiches.

"Sister, this is really very kind of you. I am hungry. Tell me though, why you? Why did someone cut off hands and feet and leave them at your door?"

"I've been wondering the same thing."

"It would help me if you could tell me about your work."

She rotated the white mug against the palm of her left hand thoughtfully, then looked up smiling. "Well . . . we consider ourselves a fairly modern community, combining the contemplative life with the active. We are a contemplative congregation in that we spend long hours in silent prayer and chanting, and, we recite the Divine Office as priests do. You can do nothing, you know, for your fellow man unless your own house is in order." She gave him a long searching look.

"When I say we try to be a community for a modern time, I will try to explain what I mean. We feel that people lose something sequestered interminably within these walls. Call it challenge, call it upheaval. They lose what they shouldn't, and they don't lose what they should. For every three years we spend cloistered from the world, we spend a year actively engaged in outside work.

"Over the years the active component has changed. We live in very turbulent times. Years ago for example, it may not have been common knowledge outside the church, but since it is no longer a large issue I can tell you, there were many alcoholic priests. We opened and ran homes for these men; you might call them hostels.

33

"Theirs was a truly superhuman task. More often than not, especially in some of our northern parishes, they were completely isolated, without human warmth and backup. Quite often they had no deep life of prayer. Insufficient emphasis was put on it during their seminary days. Then, they did not have it to fall back on in time of stress. We ran six houses here in New York.

"When the country got itself involved in the Korean 'conflict,' a trickle of people began seeking asylum. It began imperceptibly. We put them in with the fathers who were drying out at the hostels." She smiled, remembering. "There was no place else to put them. Some of the fathers stayed on." She gave a throaty laugh that brought a madcap devilishness to her eyes. "They became involved in a broad kind of social work. Many said it kept them off the drink better than AA.

"Well . . . the Korean conflict resolved, so to speak . . ." She hesitated, gathering her thoughts. "The trickle grew to a flood. Viet Nam catapulted us into the East. Before we had time to plan, we had Vietnamese children arriving in groups of six and eight. All that air traffic over Laos! Laotians joined the flood in the late sixties. Such shattered bodies!"

Eli ate in silence for a longtime. When he had completely finished a second thick sandwich, he picked up the still hot coffee pot, put it into the drawer and pushed it forward.

"Sister, warm up your coffee." She looked at him distractedly. "Coffee," he said again. She did what he suggested, and he sat in silence while she drank.

She seemed to have gathered herself up. "Many groups stepped forward with help for the children. The Protestant churches were marvelous, Bishops Relief . . . , well, you know as well as I what has happened in Cambodia. What the

Khmer Rouge have done to their own is . . ." She was at a loss to find words for the massacre of one million Cambodians. "By then we had very well established lines of transport. We have a few dozen Cambodian families re-established across the state, a dozen in the parish. I'm afraid it was merely a drop in the bucket."

He felt exhausted and realized he was sitting on the edge of his chair, straining forward as she spoke.

"We now have nine houses outside engaged in work, and we always seem to have the numbers necessary to staff them while keeping the powerhouse going here."

"Sister, do you have enemies?"

"The enemy within." He heard it distinctly, but when he asked her to repeat what she had said she looked sheepish. "There are always forces at work pulling and tugging. We get a few crank calls every month warning us Armageddon is upon us. Now and then someone scales the fence, usually a youth on a dare. Twice though, sisters have been molested; we no longer use the garden after dark. People sometimes disagree, say we should stay in the monastery and say our prayers. Some of our own feel that way. People tend to become zealots when they cannot find a door out of their own limited selves. There are many zealots in the world, Detective.

"While our country was actively involved fighting in Asia, some of the neighborhood had missing sons, dead sons and daughters. It was difficult for them to watch us care for, help, and heal Asian children." She stopped.

How can you know another soul, Eli wondered, except via some kind of correspondence, something shared. He knew this woman; he could see the center of her being. This was not good sex or the shared exhilaration of birthing a child. This was not fighting side by side, nor being wounded together. All these were familiar to him. He had spoken to her twice. Yet something wrestled between them. He thought of Jacob struggling with the angel. He fought well did he not? What did the contest prove? Eli didn't remember.

They did not glance at each other as he shuffled the plates through the drawer and she piled them on the tray. When he did look up to say good-bye she stood quite erect, her eyes calm, and it seemed she looked a little bit amused.

Chapter Four

Yesterday's snow is a thin coverlet-cloud being drawn off eastward. Frost advancing deeper into the earth, the ash bends casting a darker shade of green through the jade bulblets by the window.

There is a barely perceptible shifting of weight in the man at the center of the room. His right arm, hand in a soft curve, follows the drop in weight to the foot. Simultaneously . . . slowly . . . the left knee follows the left arm upwards.

'Golden cock stands on left leg' holds for long effortless moments, flows onward, every part of the lean sinewy frame a study in synergism. Control of the active by means of the quiet.

Weight shifts. The torso drifts counterclockwise, the limbs clockwise. A heel touches bare wood. An arm folds, a palm falls open and one curves downward. A long, slow kick toes the northwest wind.

He told me he began studying karate on Mott St. between Prince and Spring. A young detective and his partner, giving chase to a pair of hoods from Little Italy, encountering the usual clog of deliveries on Houston, then Mulberry, were nevertheless advancing on what, though not upper family, was definitely tangential offshoot.

Eastward on Prince, turning south onto Mott, they sprinted in youthful abandon, just about to touch tail when an Asian woman stumbled screaming from a Chinese laundry, quite ferociously howling at the threshold stage of childbirth. Now all police officers are given basic classroom training in emergency birth, but this is no preparation.

Those who have had even one experiential meeting with this threshold will tell you that a woman is madly crazed to find a human arm to cling to while the gates of life open those last few crucial centimetres and the baby begins its descent. Brief sometimes. Always overwhelming. They had no familiarity with the dialect; it was not necessary. To their chagrin, the faces on the street remained impassive.

In the instantaneous decision-making so characteristic of youths of noble lineage, he and his partner bent to the woman and watched the thugs race southeast. But as the partner ran to the laundry for a phone, quickly surmising that he could run faster, and the woman, her belly heaving mountains beneath the thin summer frock, clung to Eli, he looked off somewhat ruefully down the street.

One man leapt between the moving cars to join the other in front of drab, brown, old St. Pat's. He watched a thin figure detach itself from the front entranceway. A silhouette against the rising heat, it set about dancing on the hot pavement.

An arm pushed forward while a leg shot out. A curved palm caught an Italian nose. Eli heard the crush of cartilage over the panting of the woman in his arms. A foot flashing unmercifully high caught the second. It happened so fast. Effortless, it looked like a dance.

The woman screamed louder than before. She dug her nails deep in his left arm. There was a great liquid gush. His right hand held a wizened, bloody thing with an erect penis and swollen balls. Wanting to laugh out loud, he caught himself. Becoming thoughtful, he held the baby in two hands. As the woman loosed his left, he looped the cord over his wrist and handed him carefully up to his mother. Her eyes declared him beautiful.

He looked up to see a Chinese gentleman with jet black hair prop one of the thugs on a pile of turds by a hydrant. The other he put against the first's back. Taking a roll of what looked like salt water tackle from his pocket, he bound them there, bowed deeply in Eli's direction, turned and walked away.

Taekwondo was offered that year at Two-Forty Centre St. behind the five statues representing the five boroughs in three, large, unused rooms. The predominantly Irish New York cop gave it barely a passing nod. He enrolled. One evening, after studying three years, he arrived early and caught a group working out in Goju.

The footwork, lightning fast, reminded him of the man on the street. He switched and earned his black belt in Goju Karate.

One evening when I was twelve he told me he'd watched a Kung Fu master from mainland China perform in a dojo in downtown Yonkers. He described the man's movements as flowing spirals, without straight thrust, without rigid line. He drew the yin yang symbol whirling within its circle. Then he asked me and my sister to double up on a bedroom. Every family should have an empty room for practice. I don't remember minding too much, though my sister borrowed and never returned my clothes and this sudden proximity gave her increased opportunity, because he spent so much time teaching us. In junior high we knew how to stop the action we did not yet know how to start.

When I learned all one hundred and twenty-eight movements of Tai Chi Chuan, he gave me these words of Ch'en Ch'ang Hsing: "In Tai Chi Chuan you will find semblance of an eagle flying, fish in the deep sea, full of life and vitality . . . mysterious is the essence of Tai Chi Chuan . . . it is a game fit for the immortals."

At 'woman-works-shuttles' Eli noted the slowed-up tempo, a dust ball lay unmoving on the wood less than a foot away.

Laurence Van de Post says the truer the movement, and the greater its content, the greater the swing of the universal pendulum.

A man of fifty-five becomes more diffuse. Hischazkus changes, from the younger man's stubborn, self-propelling ego-core to something immeasurably finer. True hischazkus, a strengthening, a divine spark, would see him through.

His body, slowed, off-balance, was not the problem mind made of it. Reveling in the art of change, it used the art of movement to visit the mountains. His body knew where the spirits lived exhaling Chi. He hadn't need of a particularly large apartment, just one capacious enough to provide him with an empty room with a good level wood floor. He'd known the moment he came through the door: the light pouring through the turret windows, the oak flooring in the long room to the left of the kitchen, the bright room off to the right.

Eli closed the door behind him as he stepped into the warmth of the tower room. He walked over and put coffee on the small gas range to perc. A square table with two chairs fit neatly in the window bay. At the opposite end a heavy, sagging armchair, squat beside a floor-to-ceiling bookcase, held the rumpled pages of Sunday's *Times*. He built the bookcase, two of them, (one in the bedroom just like this one), after convincing Mrs. Poole they would be welcome improvements to her property. He had never liked bureaus, the one in the bedroom told at a glance when it was wash day. Taking up one whole wall, it held the stereo and a couple of lamps. A double bed and an old comfortable lazy-boy were the only items of furniture.

Drinking the coffee very hot and very black he knew that

someone had seen the delivery at Annunciation Monastery a week ago.

He let the knowledge sit there as if unobserved. And while he ignored it with his brain he felt the Chi drift in like fog. He did not visualize the monastery. He did not recall the cookie cutter houses with their distinctive trim, nor the surrounding streets. He drifted with the fog.

"I'm not saying mandarin manners will solve the case . . ." He was interrupted. "I agree . . . much more, yes . . . yes . . . But Janah is." He flicked his forefinger along the spine of his cigar sending a directly aimed snowfall on the right boob. He'd been working on burying the two symmetrical pink mounds on the cutesy ashtray while listening to the captain grumble about the heat he was under from the mayor, the archdiocese, the commissioner, the Asian delegation, the press. The surface of one tit disappeared. Three large flakes with no place to lie slid down the volcano.

"He's got Fay and Bathesday. Of course. Of course! He works best though . . ." He was interrupted again. This time he listened to a tirade on prima donnas. When it petered out he ventured, "Captain, remember Cadilluci? Joe Razetton? The Dewey multiple murders? Lone bird ain't bad." He looked up.

Lone bird looked like thoughtful stork standing in open door wearing a charcoal grey suit and white turtleneck, a dark grey overcoat hung on his left arm. Motioning Eli in, his hand scattered the ash like fairy godmothers shake stardust.

No Asian deaths from hemorrhage due to mutilation on the East coast." The lieutenant delivered this announcement to his senior detective while lowering the phone to its cradle. "And that," bowing to the phone, "as you've probably guessed was the captain. He wanted to make sure we have enough help on this." Eli was silent. The 'we' sounded conspiratorial. "He'll raise the damned and the dead and deliver them here . . . if we want help." A searching look met Eli. "He wanted assurances." Eli nodded, an unspoken agreement between them and went out to look for John Fay and Walt Bathesday. Dapper, the lieutenant thought, breaks all stereotypes. He watched the tall, thin man with the curly greying temples navigate the desks on the open floor.

Eli found John Fay perched atop his desk in a modified lotus. His whole appearance said he regarded the trip from Haight Ashbury in the late sixties to New York detective in the late eighties as humorous, at the very least. Walt Bathesday, the balding ex desk sergeant, ex Vietnam veteran, lay back in his chair, his feet on the blotter. Working with Eli Janah, one learned to wait. He had a circuitous way of thinking that the sergeant had encountered on Nam, odd to find in a Jewish-American, odd to find, and yet vaguely electrifying. He got more excitement working on a case with Janah than he'd ever got climbing into bed with a woman. He got along OK with Fay; he was a regular guy, sometimes a bit lazy. These young guys don't know what hard work is, Bath thought. Janah though, he was something else.

Eli dropped into the empty chair. "Lieutenant says we have help if we need it."

"Help? Who needs help? John and me, we finished the neighborhood canvass. Some interesting characters around those monastery walls." He chewed the inside of his cheek thoughtfully. Eli liked these two; this would be the sixth or would it be the seventh case they'd worked on together?

Bath missed very little, and Fay, because he looked as much like a detective as a kid from junior high, was privy to confidences that the other two could never elicit. Neither minded long hours, Bath, a confirmed bachelor and Fay, a recurrent on again off again with a tall, studious girl in the steno pool. Unlikely pair. Yet they had been 'getting together again' now for five years. He didn't hear about the separations, but he knew immediately from Fay's hangdog appearance when they occurred. They would understand now.

"I'm going to run a modified, door to door, myself," Eli shrugged. "Funny hunch." They nodded.

"The semi out of central sorting was an hour forty minutes late in arriving . . . carriers piled up three deep . . . I was late . . . REAL late!

"When I got here the place was runny with flashing red lights, gawkers lined the street." The man in postal uniform gestured with his chin. "Three cops made sure I was legit. Who else would be driving a stub with postal stickers?" He shook his head. "They wouldn't let me near the turn. Told me to deliver the mail to the side door. What a mess. Can you believe all this?"

Eli glanced over the man's shoulder. When the red, white and blue truck arrived, he had been standing before the massive, silent sightlessness of the Monastery of the Annunciation, absorbed.

A mountain would be surrounded by Chi of great gentleness and strength. This complex of buildings was encircled by a void against which an invisible current of bile worked. The dragon's veins—as the Chinese called them—were riled, the invisible currents that flow between the hills and follow the water courses and valleys were not easeful.

As he was considering this, the little man suddenly leapt out of the postal vehicle, challenging. What was he doing here? Was he visiting? Had he business? By way of apology, after Eli silently showed his badge, the man explained that everyone in the neighborhood looked after the sisters.

The neighborhood was extremely quiet, yet according to Bath and Fay, it was not a true bedroom community, with the majority traveling off to the city for work every day. A number of students rented houses. They were occasionally the joy of a lonely widower and quite often the bane of those who were not enamored of loud stereo systems played at late hours. Quite a few retired people owned homes. For three months they became snow birds in Florida or Texas, but otherwise they liked the north.

Rows and rows of maple shade trees, now leafless, lined the road to the monastery, which looked like a beacon of peace at the end. Until you came up to it. Eli wondered if everyone felt this heaviness. Making switch-backs up and down the streets from his parked car, he encountered one man who walked a dog and didn't look at him until he passed, three toddlers in their yard, howling with glee while they threw the sand from their sandbox out onto the pavement, a young woman hanging up her wash in a red checkered man's lumber jacket and nothing else, and the Remco Oil Company man making a delivery.

Each street had seemed tranquil until it neared the hub, the monastery. He was considering the ramifications of this when the idiot mailman had arrived. While Eli was wishing he would go away, the mailman suddenly said he had deliveries and left.

The man probably took off abruptly because Eliaphus Daniel Janah turned to stone. Some would find this disconcerting. As honest as he was about his own failings, he didn't fully realize his own enigmatic quality. When the mana was upon him—he would say the Chi—he had no patience with ordinary mortals. His innate good manners, while dictating external behavior, did nothing to disguise the inner change; the power flowing through him turned his soul like a wheel in the direction it wished to go.

Now, standing beside the neat black and white sign reading Congregation of Prompt Succor, his eyes roamed over the streets. From the rise, the heads of four streets were visible, seventh and eighth on his left, first and second on his right. The remainder, unseen from this vantage point, radiated out behind the monastery outbuildings and the large black fenced enclosure.

A walkway backed each row of houses, an alley, running past various kinds of picket, chain link, and post fencing around small patios and gardens. He headed for the alley between eighth and first.

The bamboo was the color of ripe timothy. Poles eight feet tall, round as a grown woman's wrist, bound together at the knuckle with figure-eights of balled twine, enclosed two adjoining yards. A gate, also of bamboo but two feet shorter, was recessed. In this tiny alcove a sword of peachwood hung below a small cinnabar bell.

The four-foot sword gleamed. It was stained a rich burnt sienna, and light reflected off the curved tip and the carved figure of the man riding the water buffalo. Childlike, Eli stood simply before Taoist magic, feeling the joy of discovery. How apt, Lao Tzu was leaving for the West, long life awaited. Lost in thought, he waited for five minutes there under the curved bamboo lintel from which the bell hung, before the dry sound of wind through hollow tubes drifted down on his head and the gate opened inward.

He caught his breath in pleasure and looked at the figure standing before him. Barely five feet tall, an old woman in a long, yellow quilted coat smiled and said, "Inspector, welcome! Welcome to my humble home!" Her voice was a whisper of leaves across a flagstone path, the long, thin, proffered hand as light as a dried yucca pod. "I've been watching." She gestured him across the threshold. "My name is SouLin."

The pleasant, dry chuckle came from a wind rattle made of eight hollow bamboo pipes suspended from the lowest limb of a black birch. A path wound over a hint of bridge. Beside a glassy pond she said, "We take the fish inside." He bent to hear, "they look forward to it."

A miniature pine forest broke at a tumble of boulders and rough hewn stone. An avalanche. Dwarfed, spike grasses collared a stand of ten-foot bamboo trees. Very young, very labile, they circled and bowed. So many spots pleasing and restful to the eye made the garden seem like a park. He could have sworn it took them hours to walk through it to the house.

The floor of the large room overlooking the garden was covered with a thick woven mat. Low couches sprawled around a sunken hearth, pillows scattered at their sides. A latticework screen from the eight-foot ceiling to the floor made a divider for a quarter of the room; a long table of black ebony could be seen behind it.

Bold, black calligraphy had been brushed onto a wide sheet

of rice paper which in turn was attached to a linen banner, hung on a screen. He stopped before the calligraphy.

"Do you read, Inspector?"

"Madam," he smiled at her and bowed, "I have not attained the status of inspector. It is Detective Janah. As for the calligraphy, the work attributed to the Spirits of Purity and Mystery has always interested me."

Her head came out of her coat then, like a turtle heading for the sea, and she did not look so old. "A woman finding someone or something to surprise her at ninety-two is indeed lucky, don't you think Detective Janah? Would you care to read for me?" She motioned to the black figures.

Eli smiled again. "The author has remained unknown. These magic taboo characters are from the book called The Secret Methods of Eminent Spirits of Purity and Mystery. They raise the thunder and call it down upon those guilty of secret evil. It is done in a very find hand. I would say the one who brushed this communed with spirits, as only an inspired calligrapher could paint that asymmetrical, unorthodox form essential to the occult talisman."

A little sigh of pleasure escaped her lips. "Won't you sit down? Tea is ready. I will pour."

Except for a comment on the unique flavor—it reminded him of fresh bergamot—Eli drank three cups in silence, watching a leaf twirl on the bamboo in the garden.

SouLin turned to business first. "My family is very indebted to the Sisters of Prompt Succor, detective. We would not be here, but for their involvement in the world of mortal form." Her face lit, and many fined lines came together in a smile, "I would be one more dead Cambodian.

"Because of them I watch my great-grandson try to kill

himself on that wreck of a motorcycle he bought with a month's allowance and my great-granddaughter worry about being dateless because she gets such good marks in math. America has been good to us."

"You speak good English."

In a light, dry tone she spoke about the French school of her girlhood. He tried to picture her on the march from Battambang she had described previously to Bath and Fay. Her mother, father, two grown sons, and a baby girl did not make it. Four grandchildren, two wilderness-conscious cousins, an aunt and she, kept barely ahead of the Khmer Rouge. Reaching Thailand, by the Bay of Sam near Rayong, they hid without food for three days until they could connect with the boatman hired to ferry them out into the Gulf and the waiting World War I troop ship.

"But you did not come to hear me talk of time long gone." She looked intently at him. "You are searching for someone." Then, after a pause, "it has been done before, you know, death by way of hemorrhage."

"At the moment, Madam, I am not convinced we are dealing with death."

A long silence followed, during which she frankly appraised the tall, composed, well-dressed man before her. Eli was thinking, she is not a person whose hand will be forced, Janah. No matter how vigorously you stir this pot there will be no uncontrolled splashing. She does not have to account to anyone for herself. You can sit here all day drinking this delicious tea and only get a full bladder.

She came to a decision. "Detective, my children are very solicitous for my well being. They feel I can no longer climb the stairs as easily and so they have given me a lovely room on the other side of that wall looking out on the garden. One of my great-granddaughters has the little attic room that I had on the third floor when I first came to America. I would not for the world let them think I am unappreciative of their thoughtfulness. But when they are away to work and class and I am alone in the house, who is to know? I climb more slowly than before," she nodded vigorously, "but just as well. I climb to my little room and sit there watching the light change as the sun drops from its noon position. Would you care to see the view from my little room?"

Eli, grinning, looked in her eyes, liking her. By the powers above he was being given a koan by some old Zen master. Ridiculous. Off balance. Irregular and perfect. He followed her to the front of the house, then on up the stairs.

In the tiny third-floor room evidently inhabited by a teenager, SouLin crossed to the rocker by the window. Two steps carried him to her side.

"You agree the view is quite lovely?" The angled window, looking out over and past the adjoining houses, opened on a vista of slope leading to the monastery chapel. Snow hung around the grass, whereas it had melted around the sign and on the roads and paths. As he stood there, a car drove up and parked in one of the five spaces. A middle-aged woman in a blue coat and hat got out, walked to the front entrance door across the creaky board, and rang the buzzer. In thirty seconds she opened the door and went inside. He turned and looked at SouLin.

"On Tuesday, Detective Janah, between twelve noon and two p.m., I observed three individuals ring that buzzer. A young boy, probably Del Martin from the adjoining parish with their host order. His father likes the bagels the bakery on Main makes fresh every day. He often combines the errands. He was very bundled up, but I think it was he. Mrs. Henry, who often cleans the extern quarters and the chapel for the sisters. And Father Elias from St. Hilary's. There was no one else."

She evidently heard his unvoiced question. "Sometimes I nod in the sun, but it was cold and grey that day. Almost certainly, I did not sleep."

Chapter Five

St. Hilary's was a monolith dating from the Church's love affair with undefined grey granite, large blocks of it. Eli's timing was lousy, and as he turned off Lawrence onto Rigby a round matron wearing a flaming orange vest atop her coat leapt out brandishing a big red stop sign. He pressed down instantly on the brakes; even so the sign came perilously close to being squashed against the snout where it swayed like a drunken effigy.

He had ample time to look the scene over as six buses rocked and rolled away from the curb spilling exhaust in great clouds on the waiting cars. A series of twelve broad stone steps set the church up and back away from the activity and a string of shops faced them. On the right, flanking Hilary's, a grey granite rectory, on the left a three-storey school, also grey granite. Modest brick homes took on from there.

A sign between the church and school with an arrow pointing back along the corridor read, Parking. As soon as the crossing guard had removed herself and her sign to the curb he flicked the Sentra's directionals right and pulled in.

Drawing into a space on the macadam behind Hilary's curved high altar, he could see part of the rectory's back door.

A square, no-nonsense sort of building, it looked like it had fallen squat from the side bell tower. It seemed all grey and dumpy, except the gate posts.

At the right rear corner of the rectory a dark pair of squared six by sixes, five feet high, faced the macadam with its array of cars, gate posts without a gate. And—if it was the entrance to a garden—without a garden.

But there may have been one sometime before. He eyed the macadam and was about to pass on along the walkway when one of the posts caught his eye. He peered at it, then ran his hand down the smooth old wood, his hand flashing great blue herons to his brain, his fingers telling the great long-toed track of the blue. He laughed to himself . . . his eyes telling him he had his hand on the tiger root.

The calligraphy had been burned deep into the wood some years before, edges of the letters were no longer sharp; they were charcoal-coated with soot and grime. Still, the two-inch high characters were decipherable. A convocation in mirror image, it called home the soul of one who had died away from home.

With his hand resting on the Oriental letters, his eyes took in the efficient lines of the church. What a strange place to find twin tigers! The tinkle of the wind chimes wafted across from the enclosed back porch of the rectory. He hesitated, feeling for something he could not name, then continued along the path to the front door and rang the bell.

A tall man with a pronounced stoop answered, wearing a checkered shirt and jeans. He broke immediately into an explanation: Mrs. Berens had gone to the store, something she needed for dinner . . . and then stopped abruptly. He recognizes me, Eli thought. There was a moment of unsteadiness on the priest's part, then a rapid shift of frames and he was the simple prelate caught with his sleeves up in the middle of a job, opening his door to a stranger.

"I'm Father Elias, can I help you?" He was almost as tall as Janah, six feet probably, but the stoop shortened. He straightened his shoulders as he held out his hand, answering an invisible order to stand tall, shoulders back, then quickly slumped again.

"Father Elias, I'm Detective Janah, might we have a few words? Is this a bad time?"

"No, no, not at all." The words were almost boisterous. "Come in, detective." He held out his hand. Eli thought the hand could have belonged to a musician, the fingers were so fine and tapering.

Having taken it, the detective appeared disinclined to part with it, and Father Stephen Elias kept himself from pulling it back. So this was the man assigned to the case, in charge really; Danley had pointed him out the other day. He looked to be about fifty, slender and fit, no paunch. The firm grasp loosened. He crossed the threshold and didn't stumble on Mary Berens' pride. Everyone fell on that throw rug and yet Elias hadn't the nerve to get rid of it for fear of hurting her feelings. Some of his friends had lost their cooks over less.

"Come on out to the back, Detective Janah, I've been mounting a cabinet while watching a stew. Both are at crucial moments."

They passed a somber front room. A crucifix hung on a beige wall above a desk. Four moderately uncomfortable chairs stood about. A crowded bookcase. Catechism exegesis, Eli thought; he dubbed it the convert's room.

The second room they passed was an improvement. It held a big couch, two soft armchairs, and a television. A fireplace held up one wall.

It got better. The room farthest removed from the public eye was a large old farm-type kitchen, chopping block dead center, large double oven, the kind of stove the good cooks like and all around the circumference in their proper niches . . . juicer . . . toaster/grill . . . microwave. Father Elias watched Eli scan the kitchen, his eyes missing nothing, "Parishioners, you know, Christmas gifts from different groups."

An angle, a level, pliers, a set of screwdrivers, a hammer, three wood chisels, and a drill lay on the floor beside a cabinet resting on its side. Eli could count half a dozen drill holes in the wall over the microwave.

Father Elias pulled a wooden rocker forward to the chop block which was empty except for a neat pile of wood screws. "Please sit down," he reached out behind him for another chair from the table foursome, "How can I help?" Eli, always listening to the meaning behind the words heard, 'Well, I guess we have to get on with it.'

"Father, I understand you say Mass for the sisters at the Monastery of the Annunciation. I'm investigating the all too human hands and feet that were left at the monastery recently. The sisters," he did not identify Damian by name, but it was she who had told him, "tell me you are their chaplain. Could you tell me what your duties are and how often they take you over?

"I took over the chaplaincy when Monsignor O'Reilly died. That was seven years ago. I say daily Mass at seven a.m. On Fridays I hear confessions starting after Mass. Occasionally, I finish as the Angelus rings at noon, but usually to hear the community takes until two or three p.m. I give Benediction every Sunday at three . . . oh yes, and also on the first Thursday of the month." He stopped and was silent. Eli, who was writing all this down, finished, looked it over and made no move to fill the silence.

Finally, without looking up, Eli said "And were you at the monastery, Father, on the afternoon in question?" At this point, all the papers had published something on the donation that had been made to the Sisters of Prompt Succor. He doubted there was a single person in the United States who did not know the exact date and time of arrival of those hands and feet.

The priest, however, said, "That would be Tuesday past?" The detective looked up then, nodding. "I had no call to go back. I left at eight-thirty after Mass. Walked to St. Hilary's, need the exercise, you know how it is." He patted his belt conspiratorially.

"How is that?" Eli did not know what spark of annoyance made him say that.

"Elias looked nonplussed. "Well, you know, everything slides to the middle." He flashed two palms as if he were about to go into an Al Jolson number or call a truce.

Eli made his next question softer. "It looks like a big parish, Father, how do you manage? From what I have here," he glanced down at the notebook, "you give quite a large block of time to the monastery. I, of course, am an outsider . . . but how. . . ?"

"Not enough hours in the day huh, Detective? I know what you mean. I find time. That group of nuns is really amazing, the work they do . . ." he stopped as if he couldn't find the words to describe the work or the extent of it. "O'Reilly, up

55

until the end, carried most of the monastery. He insisted, it was his baby. I took it on thinking it would be temporary." His shoulders straightened. "But I found the commitment more important than I had imagined."

He looked directly at Eli. "Father Allen and Father Strisbel take an extra portion of the parish obligations. Jeff Allen takes over the monastery when I'm out of town."

Eli had been assessing the man as he talked. Competent. Sensitive hands, strong chin. As the priest leaned forward and clasped his hands over his knees, Eli watched a nerve jump at the angle where the mandible joins the bony socket; under strain.

"Holy Mother of God the stew!" Elias leapt for the pot where the contents were making little spitting and hissing sounds. He grabbed the pot off the burner without a holder and slapped his hand hard on his thigh, reaching quickly for a large spoon with the other. Making digging motions into the stew he tried to stir it. "Almost . . . but not quite." Suddenly, he picked up the kettle and poured a huge splash of water into the goulash. He slowly, laboriously stirred, peering at it all the time. "I don't see . . . any . . . real charred evidence . . . she'll never know, where's the Worcestershire? . . . With his left hand he swung the cabinet door open . . . finger pointing along a double row of condiments until the found the Lea and Perrins. Resting the spoon a moment he unscrewed the cap, upended it and shook it well half a dozen times. Tasting this, he hesitated, then strode to the refrigerator where he found the ketchup in the door. Only then did he seem to remember Eli sitting by the chop block quietly watching. "Great disguise" he waved the bottle, "they burn it you know." Six strong dollops hit the stew and quickly disappeared with a few swipes of the spoon. Tasting again, he seemed satisfied and rested against the stove.

The noise behind them made both men turn. A woman was bending over a package she had just propped against the porch screen door. After rearranging her pocketbook strap on her shoulder she marched determinedly in the direction of the parking lot.

"Oh, God." This time Father Elias did not call on the mother, no one but the top dog for a situation like this. Galvanized into action, he reinserted the Worcestershire in the cabinet, slamming the door even as he was across the floor with the ketchup.

Evidence aside, he quickly ran the tap over the brown glop adhering to the stirring spoon, rubbed it with a finger, replaced it by the pot, and dropped—flashing Eli the look of a chagrined child—into the chair just in time to rise again. Eli smothered a smile. The father was now ushering a tiny woman through the door, using his back as a stop, holding two grocery bags, one in each arm, while apologizing for not having heard her.

"Mrs. Berens, may I introduce Detective Janah. He is the senior investigator on the case . . . the business at the monastery you know . . ." he ended lamely to the back of her head. The small woman with the face of a bulldog barely glanced at Eli as she sniffed the air, removed her coat, and hurried past them all in one motion. They might have been the cliffs of Tyron and the Palisades and she a barge determined to reach the Verrazano Bridge before five.

"Father, did you neglect my stew? Father, I asked you specifically . . ." the voice was deep and querulous. Any moment Eli expected her to bark. Sure enough, she gave an exasperated cough that qualified.

"The stew is fine, Mrs. Berens, just fine," Elias was saying in soothing tones.

At that point Eli had had enough of the stew. "I really must be going, Father, when would it be convenient to talk again? I think you could be of help, I've some questions about the sisters' work."

Father Elias, looking at the woman stirring the stew, then facing Eli, was the picture of a man caught between two undesirables. He managed a smile. "Any time, Detective . . . Well, Sunday afternoons are free until three and after four." The man's eyes flickered left and right, and Eli decided to leave him to the tyrant of the cooking pot.

"Why don't we say Sunday at four; I'll meet you at the monastery."

"That would be fine, I'll look for you after Benediction."

Eli could not interpret the look the little bulldog was directing toward the father. "Mrs. Berens, I would like to talk to you, too, what would be a convenient time?" The woman was definitely ugly. The look she fastened on him was also ugly; she made no effort to soften it.

"I'm very busy, Detective, I don't know nothing about what happened at the monastery."

"Routine, Mrs. Berens. I'm afraid I must talk to a lot of people in the hope that what they don't know may help us." He was aware of Father Elias' eyes on him, but he kept his fastened on the housekeeper. Patiently, insistently, he waited.

"Well . . . Tuesday's my day off. Afternoons I visit my sister. Mornings I'm free."

"Here?"

"Where else?" The little close eyes looked at him suspiciously. "My room's here. Kinda tiny it is but I don't complain."

"Tuesday morning around ten. Father, I'll see you at four on Sunday. All right if I go out this door?" As he opened the door to the porched-in area, the chimes made their discreet, tinkling sound. "By the way, how long has the parking lot been behind St. Hilary's?" Father Elias looked puzzled. "I gather you had a garden at one time."

"Yes." The priest hesitated, "but how did you know? There was a garden when I was sent here. Because of the parking crush on Sundays, we blacktopped it." He seemed to be thinking. "I guess we covered it over the year Monsignor died."

"Gateposts?" Eli pointed out the side window to the dark pillars.

The priest squared his shoulders, "It didn't seem necessary to uproot them too."

"Until Sunday then."

Fitting his keys into the ignition of his car, he wondered what a man had to do to keep a cook. The good father had known very well who he was; he had not introduced himself as senior detective. The source of that information was probably Bishop Danley. He wondered what else the bishop had said to the two prelates. And he wondered where the link was.

Chapter Six

"John, find out what you can about Father Stephen Elias of St. Hilary's." Fay, perched atop a desk, wrote something in a black spiral notebook. "And while you're at it check out Fathers Allen and Strisbel."

"The three blackbirds in the pie huh?" Fay chuckled softly at his own joke and wrote again.

"And Bath," Eli swung to his right, "you check out Danley, that's Bishop Danley."

"Yo," Bath signaled.

"And a ten-year-old named Del Martin who attends the next parish over. Been told he runs errands for the Monsignor there, gets his breads here." Bath and Fay watched him with mock round eyes. Sheepishly, Eli explained, "That's a kinda catch-all for the altar hosts. The sisters bake them and sell to the parishes . . ." His voice trailed off. "Come off it you two, I'm Jewish . . . even if I don't practice."

"I'll take the kid," Fay said and threw a folded paper at Bath when he came back with "same age."

"Walt, you may as well take the cleric who came along with the bishop to the exorcism of the Annunciation last Wednesday. John," Eli motioned to Fay, "last, for now. A Mrs. Henry. She cleans the extern quarters of the monastery for the sisters. We have a witness who thinks either the kid, the housekeeper, or Father Elias made the delivery; she saw all three go in there between noon and two p.m. last Tuesday." Fay gave a low whistle toward the ceiling.

"Nefarious is not always the right adjective. By definition, occult can mean anything hidden from normal understanding. We consider occult and metaphysics interchangeable today." She smiled. "Did you know that until the eighteenth century occult belief systems were accepted at all societal levels?"

Marion Rasille, tiny, dark, vivacious, probably early forties, was very attractive. She rested her chin on her clasped hands, elbows squarely on the table. "I would have said yes to dinner you know." He was so startled he didn't answer.

She picked up the chain again as easily as she dropped the stitch. "Ritual magic orders are secretive. Rosicrucianism, Spiritualism, Theosophy, Anthroposophy . . . In each of these you have to earn the magic knowledge through specific training. Your consciousness has to be awakened first."

Eli watched and listened with a curiously rising heat in his groin. She had chosen the restaurant. The tables were ridiculously intimate. No way he could eat the quiche feeling the heat of her with his knees.

And so he fumbled and finally eased them out in time to trip up a waiter hurrying by with a bottle and two wine glasses on a small tray. Only his speed—one hand before the waiter's waist, one on his spine—kept the man on his feet. The glasses jiggled. The bottle wove a curious pattern and settled.

Before a class of law enforcement people he had heard she

was Ms. Cool personified. He was being offered something as hot as Giordo's chicken wings. It surprised him to know he wanted that hot meal very much.

The laughing, brown eyes with the slight Asiatic narrowing at the outer canthus did not swerve from his face.

"There is a current revival?" he asked.

"Definitely, Taking part of the body of a person is the commonest way of working white or black magic on them." She toyed with the teaspoon. "This doesn't seem to have the earmarks of cult though."

Her eyes watched his hands, as they had when he tore the hot, long loaves of fresh bread apart, her absorption telling him quite clearly what she imagined those hands doing to her.

"Would you like coffee?" Eli asked. She shook her head. "You've helped clear some misinformation I've acquired," he told her. She shrugged her shapely shoulders in apparent nonchalance, the soft, pink material tucking itself provocatively in the marked cleft between her breasts for long endearing moments.

The shoulders, when they finally squared, seemed to blow the round breasts halfway across the table; hard nipples poked at him through the fuzzy cloth. She couldn't be wearing a bra. If she was, it wasn't much.

Papa, you want hutzpah? *This* is hutzpah. No one is shlomei emunah—whole hearted in their faith—before this! No one!

"As I said, it doesn't have the earmarks of cult." Her brows flew down like graceful wings. "Cult killers don't publicize. Not like this." She was thoughtful for a few moments. "Although humans make rituals like they make love . . . in an infinite number of variations . . .

"Have there been warnings? Festering angers? Have the

good sisters made enemies? You say none of the repatriot families have been threatened or harmed?" Her mouth pursed like a soft bud, the thought of crushing it against his own was stronger than most of the simmering hatreds he had encountered in his long career.

By that time, his mind made up, it was merely a matter of willing his body to quiet down and since will had never gotten him anywhere, he kept his mind on the case. Thinking of the monastery turn and the sisters' dismay he stood abruptly, "Are you quite sure you don't want dessert?"

"Yes."

He reached across and pulled her to her feet. "Let's go then."

"Where?"

"Yours or mine . . . whichever's closest."

The smile she gave him made him stiffen anew. "I'll meet you in the car. I have to stop at the ladies' room."

The motor was idling easy when she came out the side door of Pierre's. He leaned over and thrust the door open for her.

"How about mine," she said, "it's only two blocks." She laughed like a child opening a present when she slid her warm fingers between his thighs and found him hard.

Turning the car onto Baily, he asked himself again what he was doing. In the last three years he could not recall a woman who had even warmed him. How often he had encountered the ego's assault on his spartan, rabbinical life saying, 'show me desire, I'll follow!' Now, in the face of a devouring desire, some part of him was splitting off, quoting Dionysius. Not knowing is the most intimate. Then, a great intimacy is *not* what I want now, he replied. I lust after this woman!

At the door to Marion's apartment, while she turned the

keys in two separate locks, he slipped off her coat. Placing his hands under her sweater, he did what he wanted to do back at the restaurant, ease thin lace up over her nipples, fill his hands with the two large, heavy breasts until the nipples were like rock. Tracing her rib cage with a finger and then around to her spine and down the hollow, he unhooked her skirt. It slid to her knees. Slowly, very slowly, Eli pulled the silk slip down over her belly and then down past her hips. He dug his hands in the curly warm fur. She wore no panties, only a garter belt with its snug, black lace elastic running loosely down each thigh.

She uttered a sigh, sagging backward. Such a lovely sight, he thought, pocketbook, skirt, coat on the floor, her slip down around her ankles, the pink sweater with the bra rolled up inside around her throat like a scarf, exposed, round, erect breasts, naked belly except for the low garter belt and stockings.

Picking her up, arms cradling perfect smooth buttocks, he slowly opened the door. Holding her exposed out into the hallway for all the world to see, kissing her, he slowly kicked each item of clothing, including the pocketbook, behind them into the apartment.

She was so wet when he finally entered her that they slid apart laughing repeatedly. But before that, in each pinned position that had leapt uninhibitedly to his inner eye, he brought her to climax after climax. He dared his flesh; how long can you stay hard for this woman and me? How long? How long? He brought her to climax again. How long? And again. And how long? Until their two bodies glistened and shone and he felt like howling.

She was whispering something; he leaned close to hear. She

was whispering 'please' over and over again. He crossed her legs then and buried himself deep.

"Well!" She lay on her left side before the couch on the thick white pile rug; they hadn't made it to the bedroom. "Well well" eyes wide and serious, no laughter lurking near the corners now. "So they were wrong."

"Who? About what?" He rolled over on his back conscious of his limp penis slipping through three inches of wet shag; the fibers of the rug moved their tendrils like underwater weeds.

Hitting the carpet between them with his palm, "You realize this is going to smell like fish wrappers." It was not a question.

She answered both. "It can be washed. Department gossips." He was silent. "The 'vine' says Eliaphus Daniel Janah never plays around." She knew his whole name.

"I wasn't."

"What?"

"Playing around." He slipped his long fingers in her hot, wet cunt, "I was playing here." She took a deep breath and he was aware of her vagina shortening and then deepening slowly but surely as she let the air out, drawing his hand in and upward.

"What caused all that?" She tried to sound light.

"All what?"

"All that passion."

With his hand within her he screwed up his eyes, seemingly absorbed in the ceiling. "Meaning is more important than cause." Suddenly, as if to forestall further questioning, not sure what the afternoon had meant, he withdrew his hand, fondling her thigh with wet fingers. "You."

She started to rise, then. "I could use something to drink, how about you?" His hand caught in the black lace garter running down her left buttock. Halfway to her feet, struggling against the pull, he let it snap. Red shot in streaks out from the black. He lunged, caught both black garters again, pulled, and as his weight dropped to the floor, let them fly. She gasped, grabbing for her bottom. In one swift move, he brought her down on the carpet easily.

She didn't cry, but struggled, breathing hard and fast, as he draped one thigh over her waist to keep her in place, and pulled the garter straps high, conscious all the while he was hard as a rock, aching like a teenager.

At each rebound of the elastic she whimpered, and the flush increased until her perfect buttocks were like two smooth, ripe raspberries.

Sliding his hand down the cleft was like driving in warm jello. He drew it out dripping and put the left one in just as deep, spreading the moisture up and back over the two hot mounds.

She groaned each time he dipped his hand, first one forefinger, then the other, making loving circles around the winking eye, and when she was thoroughly ready, changing position rapidly, he took her from behind with one hand encircling her groin, fingering her swollen, retracted clitoris.

The coroner's offices, along with the City Assessor, Business Permits and Regulatory Assistance, Child Abuse and Maltreatment, Code Enforcement and Dog Control, occupied a large old mansion that looked like it came right off the set of Witches of Eastwick. A low brick structure had been attached to one side; here Eli found Manny Bozeman.

"It's almost four. I was about to give up and go home, figured I'd call you tomorrow at the apartment."

"Got back to the desk later than expected. Came right over when I saw your note."

Bozeman looked at Janah for a long, silent minute. Was there a rare gruff note in his voice? Maybe he was tired, everyone was relieved to have Friday come around. Still, he didn't look tired; he looked ten years younger. He let it go.

"Got some interesting tidbits on your hands and feet."

Eli, checking first that it was clean and dry, dropped onto the rim of one of the two stainless steel autopsy tables. "Shoot."

Bozeman took four steps to the wall of freezer drawers and pulled the last open. More than a drawer, this cubicle at five feet was high enough to enclose a stretcher and Manny wheeled it to Eli's knees. He looked down on the three hands and three feet as Bozeman heaved himself with no finesse up on the opposite table.

"First hand, you may wanna take notes." He waited while Eli drew a notebook from an inside overcoat pocket. "The first hand has been in Formalin for almost two years." He pointed at this horror, the hand looking like a hook or a crooked claw as if reaching from a grave. "The hand of a seventy-five year old woman. Notice the deformity. It's characterized by hyperextension of the metacarpophalangeal joints," he gestured to the area closest to the severed wrist, "and flexion of interphalangeal articulation," he pointed to the fingers. "Grabs at ya, huh? Probably caused by a median nerve injury. From the degree of contracture I calculate the woman received the injury in her early fifties.

"Second hand, woman's, forty-four years old, was fresh. The

67

lady lost it within the past month. Notice the nails; they look like spoons, that's why they call them spoonnails. They're not like normal nails at all, they're concave. Koilonychia." He caught Eli looking at him with a blank expression, "k o i l o n y c h i a, he spelled it out. "Bet you my druthers she has iron deficiency anemia.

"The third hand was a forty-six year old male's. He chewed his cuticles, otherwise nothing special. From the degree of cellular breakdown, I'd say it's been frozen for about a year.

"This foot . . . about thirty-three, male, fresh. Very fresh. The guy is still adjusting to life without a right foot. Longitudinal arch flattens out on the floor," he sounded professorial again, "normal concavity on medial side becomes convex. I'd check his shoes for wear on the inner sides of the soles and heels.

"Second foot, frozen about a year, seventy-six, male," he pointed to the magnificence of toe. "First, I thought Haberdens . . . but I remembered old Cussach poking me in the ribs," his voice took on a watery, high-pitched quality, "'Come on, Bozeman, what mimics Haberdens . . . what mimics?' Professor . . . anatomy lab in med school," he explained to Eli's questioning look.

"Tophaceous gout!" he crowed. "It's not osteoarthritic degenerative joint disease. The gentleman has gout."

"The last foot there, eighty-six year old male, more or less, was one of the first gathered. It's been in Formalin at least two years. Nothing untoward there but age."

Eli made rapid shorthand notes by three of the entries, then looked over at Manny, "You're good!"

"Ahh . . . but that's not the real meat. Something had me

by the balls. Couldn't get rid of this nagging suspicion that I was missing something that would pull all six together."

At this point, his face took on the cherubic happiness of a Raphael descending to earth as illustrated for Milton's Paradise Lost from Hayley.

"The bones were hacked . . . nothing neat there . . . you might well call it vehement action. But! I thought I saw hemostat grooves on one arterial fragment. Well, age creeps up on all of us." He looked at Eli apologetically. "Could have been my eyes, *but* just to be sure I took a run down to Columbia. Borrowed some right fine magnification from my friend Gallerie, he's the neurosurgeon, remember?

"Hemostat, Eli, d'ya understand?" His excitement mounted. Slowly . . . pacing each word, "It took me a while but now I'm sure. Severance of every major blood vessel was by surgical . . . scalpel." Bozeman waited for Eli to grasp the full measure of his disclosure.

Eli found his mind racing. "Time obscures," Manny was almost babbling now, "vessels retract, turn to mush . . . if I hadn't seen those two little nips on the brachial on spoonnails there. . ." He gestured with his pencil and then threw up his hands helplessly.

"The radials, the ulnars, the deep," he stressed it, "the *deep* anterior interosseous in the lower arms. The dorsalis pedis," the Latin was flowing like a poem, "posterior tibialis . . . the peroneals! He got the anterior peroneals where they bifurcate." He slapped the stainless steel at his side and the metal-flesh contact ricocheted around the cold room.

"Then, Janah, this guy got the veins. He left nothing to bleed. It was a labor of love." Looking at Eli's face he tried again, "Hate? He cut the radial and the median in the arm where it joins and before it anastamosises with the anterior ulnar itself. The marks were all there." There was deep professional pride in his voice.

"He caught every major branching at the saphenous. Do you know what a networking the internal and external have in the lower leg?!" Eli didn't know but looked attentive. This was not the time to open his mouth. Manny continued, "You can pull those beauties. When they're extremely varicosed you just snip and pull them out." He made little nip and tuck motions that brought a groan to Eli's lips. "They have so many branchings; the damn ancillary take over.

"Once I was sure of all this, I went back and re-ran the chemistries looking for traces of anesthesia. Fluothane . . . nothing. No halothane. No penthrane. Big zeros on chloroform, nitrous oxide, ethyl chloride, ethylene. Couldn't find the injectables either. Ketalar, brevital, pentothal. . . ? Not a thing. No one lies down for this."

"I started thinking of all the anesthetics that have come and gone. Many we don't use any more; they're too damn flammable. Tiny spark, boom! Everything blows up. Still . . . some of them are used in undeveloped countries. Boom is not as bad? Cheap."

He was almost talking to himself now, "I tried to ask myself what was cheap and plentiful. Guess what I found." He smirked.

"Cocaine! An alkaloid obtained from erthroxylin cocoa. In every single one of those specimens I found traces of cocaine hydrochloride, a local anesthetic.

"They watched while he cut off their hands and feet. The

two eldest had trouble taking it lying down. One stopped breathing. There are traces of epinephrine in the hand of the old woman, clawhand there. And the eighty-six year old gent must have gone into convulsions. I found propanol as well as cocaine." The two men were silent. A slow drip, drip from one of the scrub sinks was the only sound in the large, tiled, windowless room.

When Manny spoke again, he had calmed down appreciably. "You're looking for someone with surgeon's skills, male or female, and who, with premeditation, cut off three human hands and three human feet. These people," he waved his had over the surface of the stretcher, "did not die from this. They were not meant to. Great care was taken that they should live."

Out on Wind Hollow Road at the Monastery of the Annunciation, a fat heifer moon, silvering the bearberrry along the deserted garden paths of the enclosure, shone on the Way of the Cross, marking twelve stations of indistinct character.

Penetrating the overhang, it fell to the white marble forehead of the statue of the Immaculate Conception where it fired the lowered eyelids. When the intermittent wind moved the boughs, this triangle winked a flickering message to the sky crescent.

"Miserere mei, Deus secundum magnam misericordiam tuam" . . . the women's voices rose and fell reciting Psalm Fifty-one. "Have mercy on me, O God, according to Thy great mercy."

In the lightness of the chapel there was no light from the garden or the altar. The shades had been drawn tight to the sill, and the tiny red vigil on guard in the sanctuary was too feeble to throw even the tiniest gleam back upon the gathered community.

"Et secumdum multitudinem miserationum dele iniquitatem meam." A steady, papery sound wove through the chanting. A horde of locusts nibbled and crunched their way through young chick peas on an Iowa farm. Hard, waxed knotted cords fell on bare buttocks. "And according to the multitude of Thy tender mercies . . ." Sister Damian swung harder . . . "blot out mine iniquity, O God!"

Chapter Seven

Sister Damian stretched the fine linen out against the light. She had been staring at it for ten minutes, ever since Detective Janah had called insisting they speak. It was imperative, he declared, when she told him that Saturday was filled with too many activities and there was no time. She recognized the unalterable force, she had been this way once. Ten minutes . . . fifteen minutes . . . he bargained and finally kept her there for twenty-five precious minutes. Why the questions about Father Elias, Mrs. Henry, and Del Martin? It was too much.

She had unplugged the phone and taken it around to the west wing, plugged it into the sacristy knowing Ellen needed the speak, then taken it back again when he hung up. She felt like a dolt; what had she been doing . . . something hadn't been quite right with the vestment, but she was having difficulty remembering what it was?

A thin stream of light shone down at the corners of the alb! She had envisioned the light just above the grape clusters and the chalice. Relieved, she placed the linen on a padded surface at the end of the work table and directed the seventy-five watt bulb on the area in question.

Snip. A thread was interrupted, followed carefully along its tract, checked and double checked. Sure it was the same thread, it was snipped again. Holding the fabric snugly, this one was drawn firmly, but gently from the rest. Standing back, she eyed it and decided two would be better. Removing the second linen thread was easier. She then crooked a foot under a stool and dragged it near. Laying the hand-loomed Irish linen over a raised knee, she started with tiny invisible stitches to build the windows.

The alb, part of the new vestments promised Bishop Danley for Christmas, had been just the work needed to completely occupy this morning. It was as good as being alone working opposite Constance. Engrossed in running up the ends of an altar cloth, she never looked up.

'Rorate caeli desuper et nubes pluant justum.' Drop down dew, ye heavens from above . . . the words from the morning's Introit were like balm, a benediction. She let the Mass of the Blessed Virgin wash over her again.

They were going through some hard times; it never rains but it pours. Was it Teresa, foundress of the shoeless Carmelites, that told her sisters not to blame it on the times? She smiled to herself, you never were one to soften the truth! She thrust that at Teresa and felt better. Even creaking over the Spanish countryside in those go-west wagons you were one strong lady.

She had wanted to get as much done on the vestment as possible, hoping to be free and unencumbered to help set up for the conference of religious convening that afternoon. Hope was high for some real dialogue. There were those who felt the letter of the law was sacrosanct and those who believed superiors, anointed with the oil of office at election, held the Spirit's blessing and power of interpretation when it came to the rules and by-laws.

A vow of obedience, to her way of thinking, was a vow of obedience. You obeyed your superiors no matter what, otherwise why take it? She did not agree with everything Mother Michaels was doing. And she was grateful she had not made habit a matter of obedience. But she could not see this incessant questioning of her pronouncements as anything but disruptive. A lot of ego! They said it was ecumenical. Ecumenical bosh! It wasn't anything but EGO in capital letters. Holier than God some of them.

Lord, when will you zap us like you did Augustine? So that we realize what you really think of our very important matters. Turn us around! She found herself moaning this last thought out loud and smiled a quick apology to Constance's raised eyes.

"If The Lord was a dirty old man," a great intake of breath surged through the conference room, "he might derive something from the practice." A dozen older sisters ducked their heads and covered their ears; what they were hearing was unbearable. One had tears in her eyes. She looked across the table, her lips silently forming the words of the rosary she thumbed beneath the table.

"With all due respect, Reverend Mother, I refuse to lift my skirt, lower my pants, and beat myself on the bare bottom. It's a dated, inquisitional practice. It has no psychological soundness. Let Luke draw blood!" This last she threw across at the lips mouthing Hail Mary full of grace.

A generous round of support flew to the silent figure saying her rosary. Yes there were stains difficult to remove; those on wash detail would attest to that. And some finding themselves unfortunately in line, asked to change places in chapel. The new young Sister Resignation hadn't caught on yet. She thought her own fervor sprinkled the dark and slipped in, early Saturday mornings, to drip hydrogen peroxide on her immediate floor.

Michaels, looking over the high-ceilinged refectory, with its great peaked beams, felt very tired. This series of weekend conferences had been in planning for six months. If this first day was any indication . . . she shook her head inwardly in exasperation.

Encouraging frankness—for how, unless they spoke honestly about their constitutions could they interpret them for their times—she hadn't bargained on some of the outspoken younger generation. But she was glad this particular matter of the discipline was out in the open. Attendance had been dwindling on Friday nights, and it was not written into their rule as a matter of individual conscience.

"We have made a beginning, only a beginning. Each of us is going to have to make sacrifices. I want you to search your hearts this coming week and remember we are working for the continuance and good of the congregation." She wanted them to read between these lines. She wanted them to know she had not seen anything today but trenchant selfishness. If this was their idea of dialogue, it just wouldn't do.

Some of these women belong in board rooms, she thought. Their energies are bottled up here without an outlet; they need to test their power. In lieu of that opportunity, they amass little armies of followers. If they could direct all that energy within, they would be saints.

She looked over to Ellen as sub-prioress for help. Ellen surprised her. Catching her glance, she cleared her throat, and in her usual coloratura soprano, "We have made a start, let us be grateful. Before we part, I think we should air last Tuesday's incident." There was immediate and total silence. Leave it to Sister Ellen to know how to stop the angry buzzing. Thirty faces faced her corner of the table. Even Luke's mouth was stilled, the rosary recitation stopped for the first time in two hours.

"The body parts left at our turn were all Asian," Ellen began. That sounds a bit ridiculous, Michaels thought, but how else could she put it. "Six different individuals. The police do not know at this time if these people are dead. Some barbarian is maiming, possibly killing human beings. Close to home! This isn't something you might see on the evening news," she directed this last to Sister Anne and her cadre. "Which means there is some connection with our life, with our work. Has anyone heard anything? On the phone? At the turn? Any passing comments, new bitternesses? What about the black mass near the college? We all know how much filters through cloister walls." A murmur of assent went around.

"We have inquired of all our Asian families. No one seems to have heard a thing. No relatives are missing. Four men. Two women." The words dropped like a bloody ax on the room. Always a touch theatrical, Reverend Mother Michaels observed the effect. There was a long, shocked silence.

"We will keep you posted of developments." Well, that will keep attendance high, Michaels thought. Ellen continued, "A Detective Janah is in charge of the investigation. If you have any information, anything that might help . . . if you wish to talk to him, about this business of course, let Reverend

Mother or myself know and we will arrange it." She then nodded in Michaels' direction, handing over the prerogative.

Mother Michaels, listening to Sister Ellen, wondered again if she should have canceled the conferences, at least for the duration of the investigation. Friends had called and counseled her to do just that. She prayed about it long and hard and decided that you could not fold up shop just because evil hit you in the face.

Bishop Danley had argued that "this was not your ordinary evil," but he tactfully refrained from making her decision for her, a gesture that earned her gratitude. She appreciated the looseness of his control of the Congregation. Ordinary evil. Extraordinary evil. When Ellen gave her the nod she was trying to find the subtle distinction.

The large moon-faced clock on the wall read four. One third of the sisters would return to their places in the world, the remaining filtering back into the life of prayer at the monastery.

Her voice, when it broke the silence, was much softer than Sister Ellen's. "I'm sure you all agree that the individual who did this is in dire straits. As much as the six need our prayers . . . let us not forget this one. This soul must be in absolute torment." Her chin shook imperceptibly. "Go in peace."

"Paul, sweet, it's good of you to think of me, but I'm fine, truly fine. Tell Jackie I appreciate the invitation but I can't, not now. Tell her I'm between the death of a monarch and the accession of the successor." The tall, sandy-haired young man sitting opposite his mother at the round oak kitchen table did not bat an eye. He knew her.

"You should come for dinner at least. You've been here almost a week. Who have you seen?"

"Clam? Chowder?" Mir was teasing him. She struck a serious tone then, "It's not who I've seen, Love, it's what I've accomplished. Oh Paul, I'm doing such good work! You know what a drug that is. I don't want to break. The Valery article is moving right along. I've got food here."

"You haven't had the phone connected."

"I know," Mir tried to look chagrined.

"Suppose you need help? Get sick?"

His mother gave him a long, loving look that said I'm fifty, young man, not eighty! "I will have it connected, first thing this week I'll stop in at the telephone company."

"I could call for you."

"No, I'll take care of it myself, promise. But it isn't going to change anything. You needn't hit Jackie on the head, but I wish you'd break it gently and make it clear that I'm not here to babysit; I'm here to work. I love my grandson . . . I'll call Jackie after I've submitted the piece."

Snow was falling gently on the hill. It sifted through the hemlocks and flung white scarfs about the knobby ends Eli had cut one year to keep the boughs from scratching on the kitchen windows. Clam and Chowder devoured the woodpecker on the suet with their eyes. Whip-whip, whip-whip went the excitement their tails could not contain.

The first heavy snow caught her feeling strangely content. She couldn't even shake herself loose from the hill to drive down for the Sunday *Times.* She had been thinking of Valery's advice to the poet to stay out of the time, send an occasional stanza to the living. When the familiar chug of her son Paul's VW Bug made itself heard, it had roared up, made a complete turn, and came to rest ready for a quick departure, heading outward just as he had done since he was sixteen. This car, not the souped up Mustang he re-built at sixteen, was more se-date, as befits the twenty-five year old father of a young son. But his easygoing, solicitous care hadn't altered; it didn't sur-prise her that he was the first of her offspring to check on his mother.

Her daughter-in-law (Mir thought of Jackie with a measure of detached amusement) was all nervous, outgoing energy. She made Paul content. That was probably important. To Paul.

As she aged, Mom was no longer sure that contentment was so good. Maybe it was the boundaries that were becoming fuzzy, good and bad switching places in her mind. I think she left Dad because of too much unchallenging, contented security. She was sure it was a good move. She was not as sure of her reasons.

Paul's Jackie was conditioned to believe that grandparents lived for the opportunity to grandparent. Quite willing, then, was she to relin-quish Jonathan, their curious, intent, one-year-old, diaper full of creeping, crawling, leaky energy, on less than a moment's notice.

It was evident she thought Mom—unlike her own mother—deficient in essential urges, an anomaly that somehow, by the grace of God, raised five children. Probably with a lot of help.

There had not been help, yet, she had not seen any bitterness in her. She lived one side of the coin; now she lived the other. Which was heads? Which was tails? Or is that a youthful question?

"Dad's conducting the investigation at the Wind Hill Mon-astery." Eli's name provoked the usual mixture of light and dark, gratitude and bitterness. "Might be a story there." Inno-cent enough remark, he continued stirring a bit more sugar into his coffee. She couldn't tell if this was a subtle gesture at maneuvering them together. Admittedly, she had thought of it. As she did her errands for the essentials, she noticed the headlines, listened to the garage mechanic give his rendition, the checkout girl at the food market, hers. Carnage and contemplation . . . there may be a feature article there, not on Eli.

He would solve it though. Admitted expertise in subjectless simulacra . . . she had been very angry the night she threw that at him. She still could see the look of confusion. Images seemed to accumulate in him, vague feelings. He caught the wind, the synchronicity of a scent, a word, a foreboding.

And from these vagaries, he brought forth an amalgam, knowledge as firm as any rational construct logically acquired. Then he only had to prove it.

Strange, that he could be so sensitive in some things!

Dipping a cruller in her coffee, she sucked the sugared end before biting it off, "These are really good!"

"Self protection," he had checked the fridge when he came in the kitchen and gestured to it now, "I don't see all that much in there. What happened to the health nut, the woman who made all those fresh baked pastries and bread stuffs, all those casseroles and stews we had to eat?"

"She's turned." Munch . . . munch.

The energy must be going into her writing for she felt no inclination to cook; cans suddenly looked good. When she sank to TV dinners . . . then she would take notice!

"Promised Jackie I'd take Jon sledding . . . you real sure about dinner?"

"Yes." It was very, *very* nice of you to stop." She meant it. The young frame unwound itself upward, the look of pleasure telling her he heard. "Careful on the drive. Does it need ashes?" Shaking his head, he hugged her.

After he went, she stood at the side door watching through the glass dew drops as the VW made its little toy tracks down to the old furry ones. Following the drive to the street, it went winking off to the right.

She had planned to go into the City in the morning. Why not now? Nibbling on a knuckle, she glanced at the dial over the stove. There was a three o'clock train.

Two phone calls from the station . . . maybe three. Lise to care for the cats, she already had a key. Pius, to book a room. And Arthur, he'd made it quite plain he was interested. Any time, he said. She flipped the Rolodex, checking for his unlisted number.

Qualms about clergy? Mir made a monkey face at herself in the mirror of the sideboard, not when it comes to even exchange, my dear. And NOT the kind you think! She grabbed Clam up from weaving about her ankles, put her nose to the moist black one and leered, "Right? Right!" Priests, bishops, cardinals . . . men, just men. Often enough, more fucked up than ordinary men, but she could handle that.

Arthur was the one to give her the lead into the Annunciation. Valery was three quarters completed. That in itself meant she should begin researching the next.

At two-thirty, not wanting to leave the Buick at the station, she called a cab. At three, she stepped on the southbound central with her black attache case, her overnight bag, and the *Times,* hurriedly bought at the stand next to the ticket window, under an arm, just as Eli gunned the Nissan up the snowy driveway of the home he'd kept for twenty-four years.

Two sets of tracks.

He parked the car and bypassing the front, went around to the back door they had always used, on the way casting a practiced eye on the siding. Should be painted soon. Especially the trim! The garage windows look bad on the north, very bad. They looked like the carrots and radishes someone had worked over on an office party platter—all curls of festered paint. The house was Mir's now, part of the settlement, but he still felt a proprietary interest.

She was not home; he could feel it.

The second-hand Buick she bought, because she considered the color electric, was in the garage. Two sets of tracks, one narrow, one regular . . . ? She left with one of them. Who? No concern of yours anymore, Janah, leave it. Hands deep in his overcoat pockets, snow setting on his hair and shoulders, he turned about slowly, there by the back door, surveying the buried flagstones, the hemlock, the fir he had planted. No continuity, he thought. We're changing too damn fast. Maybe not fast enough.

Chapter Eight

Tops of the cloister garden hanging heavy-lidded and white over the black fence—he was early and drove slow—a dozen branches cracked and fallen outside the enclosure, snow-laden trees unable to contain the weight, touching uncircumcised ground. It all looked quite wild and beautiful.

And it's going to be some cleanup, still coming down. Parking the car on the street, he trudged through the accumulation to the heavy, dark wooden doors of the Church of the Annunciation and pulled one open.

A wave of incense struck him. He shook the snow from his hair, removed his overcoat, and stomped the excess from his shoes in the vestibule. Quietly, he opened the inner door, slipped in, and sat down in one of the rear pews.

Approximately thirty people were scattered through the semi-darkness. A blaze of light about the high altar stood in marked contrast with the rest of the church. Many candles flickered on either side of a gold throne before which Father Elias was prostrate, while a cloud of smoke rising on either side made its way forward, gained status, and engulfed the round, white circle within the gold.

Two young boys wearing white lace smocks, swung their

censors with abandon, clickety-click, the chains dangled against the brass while smoke poured from circular mouths in the metal.

Over it all, the high ethereal song . . . coming from behind the great grill left of the altar. Twenty-four feet from floor to ceiling, this grill in the church was even more impressive than the one in the speak. A curtain half-way up, extending the width, allowed the community to see the altar while remaining unseen.

After an Amen, there was a brief pause. Elias stayed where he was at the foot of the altar. Very slowly, the hymn started and Eli could make out the words 'Tantum ergo sacramentum . . . ve ne re mur cer nu i.' So paced was the delivery, so crisp the syllables, he could have written it down without knowledge of the Latin. Et an ti quum do cu men tum . . . from within the cloister wing of the church, the song rose like the cloud.

He felt surprisingly let down at Mir's absence. He hadn't called, deliberately leaving himself just enough time for it to look like a friendly hello. Casual. Nothing serious. On the way somewhere . . . It was sort of like having the rug pulled out from under your feet to have this rehearsal for nothing.

Pomp and circumstance. But curiously beautiful. There was perfect stillness among the onlookers in the church. He compared the scene before him to the inner chamber, the Holy of Holies, circumspect, guarded by angels and flaming swords. Here were a scrap of bread raised up and two little snot-nosed kids having a ball.

Eli ignored the surreptitious glances of more than one parishioner. Finally, the church empty, two young boys came side stepping down the aisle pummelling each other's nonexistent biceps. They stopped when they came even with his pew, poked each other, and tumbled through the door, leaking their smothered laughter into the vestibule.

An occasional rustle told him the nuns had remained quietly on their side of the grill. There were a series of clicks as one light after another was doused. Then, the shadowy tall figure of Father Elias came out from behind the altar, genuflected in the dim light, turned, and walked toward him.

"How many people have keys, Father?" He stood to the side as Elias pulled the outer heavy doors closed with a decisive click, locked them and straightening up, looked Janah calmly in the eye. "Only me. Sister keeps a set at the turn in case of an emergency. She can pass them out and have someone else open up. The church has been locked between services for as long as I've been here. It just does not pay to allow anyone to drift in whenever they please.

"Vandalism, theft, the homeless sleeping in the pews" . . . there was a hard edge to his voice, "you have to protect your own, Detective. When the Lord isn't able, we do it in his place. Do you want to walk?"

The two men looked down the slope at the snow falling heavily under the street light. Eli's feet had just about dried out. "Why don't we take the car, Father? How about coffee?"

As the car moved slowly away from the sprawling shadow of the Annunciation, Father Elias sat up straight, "I know just the place, take a left three blocks ahead."

Father Elias didn't act nervous. Neither man smoked. They sat at a rear table in the small cafe behind the college annex.

"You have a current passport then?"

"Yes. I made my first trip for the sisters six years ago. I couldn't fill Monsignor's shoes, he handled so many details, took such risks when it was an open fire pit over there. I did soon see why though . . . by actually standing on Cambodian soil, many arrangements were made easier. He had found that out long ago.

"The sisters have probably told you they've helped some few dozen people re-locate."

"They haven't mentioned numbers."

"I thought not," there was a look of satisfaction on Elias' face. "Those numbers run well over two thousand. Koreans . . . Vietnamese . . . Thai . . . Cambodians . . . Laotians . . . Often enough, they hated each other's guts over there . . . Did you know, detective, that Buddhism has been more successful in healing tribal war between same-skinned peoples than Christianity? I know some Vietnamese and Korean Buddhist families that are closer than most Americans."

"Did you always want to be a priest?"

"No," there was a long pause, "not always." A barely perceptible shrug dislodged the pause. "Couldn't hack the grades, great on practice, but not on theory. Have you ever known innately how to perform a task, Detective, and been unable to explain what you were doing? They want explanation, you know."

"Who?"

"The world?" Father Elias gave hiim a quizzical, half humorous look. "It is easy for me to lose myself in just about any hands-on construction."

"The cabinet?"

"Yes, that sort of thing. I'm very talented," he looked intently at thé palms of his hands outstretched on the table as if questioning them. "Sometimes, I think they have a mind of their own. I had a brother. He died a few years ago. He was the exact opposite. The only thing he ever did with his hands was catch a pigskin in the end zone. But contrary to the label most athletes get, he had a brain, got great grades. What a wonderful, sharp mind!" The sigh forced an extended exhalation.

"How did he die?"

"Slowly . . ."

Eli waited . . . "Slowly?"

"What?"

"You said, slowly?"

"Did I?" he shook his head in consternation. "He died in the Viet Nam War. I'd like more coffee, how about you?" He had risen from the table and was half way to the counter before he finished the sentence.

"You were close, you and your brother," said Eli as the Father put the two cups of steaming hot coffee down beside the empties.

"Yes."

"Any other brothers or sisters?"

"No, just us. Our folks died in a car crash when we were teenagers, just old enugh to make it on our own. We went to the same college. Dated the same girls."

"There must be a natural bitterness in losing a loved brother to the people you are now involved in helping." Elias looked at him, his steady pale eyes almost grey.

"No bitterness, Detective. One does what one has to do. Bitterness, anger . . . these boomerang. They're pointless. I'm a lucky man to be able to carry the love of Christ to the very people who killed my brother. I couldn't do it without grace. No bitterness. Great peace." He said these last words low, almost to himself, and drained his coffee cup.

"What about ill feeling in the neighborhood over the sisters' involvement in Asia?"

"I'd be lying if I said it doesn't exist. I can think of half a dozen former supporters who've switched attendance to St. Hilary's. Some of those would go farther if they could. Have you noticed on Eighth, the cluster of Vietnamese families? The Murphys, Mr. and Mrs. Keane, the Rubinskis, and old Mrs. Cooley up and sold their houses to avoid what they called the yellow plague."

"How does Bishop Danley feel about the sisters' involvement in Asia?"

Elias sat with his head bent. Eli could see the nerve jump at the mandible insert. "I think it best you ask His Reverence that, Detective."

"I will Father, I will. One last question, was it you that burned the tiger root in mirror image into the old gate posts?"

Instead of answering, the priest asked his own question. "Are you familiar with the mystic diagrams used in magic rites? Perishable, Detective, that's the key. Perishable. A reminder of the eternal change which governs the universe.

"Mystic diagrams used in magic rites, drawn on paper, burned. Evil forces sketched in dust, scattered in disarray. As perishable as we are. I burned the tiger roots when Tim was first listed missing in action."

"Your brother?" Elias nodded.

"You've been very helpful," Eli said. "I can drop you off at St. Hilary's."

"No. I'd just as soon walk."

"Are you sure?" Eli calculated almost eight miles.

For answer, Father Elias pulled his collar high, waved, thrust both of his hands in his pockets, and strode off. By the time Janah pulled the car from the curb and passed him before making his turn, the priest's hair and shoulders were white.

At that very moment, Mirari Buttrick Janah was reading a note on the lower west side of Manhattan. Great! Puglia's? Ziti? Seven p.m. He'd found her message on his answering machine and responded as she thought he would. The receptionist at Pius handed her the note with the key.

Arthur did not like Sundays, a holdover, he said, from the seminary. He called the seventh day 'dead meat' and usually scheduled a poker game. Wonder what new hand he held . . . or thought he held, that had him throwing in the old. Just boredom, my dear; he's fond of women. Fond of women in a position that does not allow it to show except in ecclesiastical, sanctioned ways. She had seen how good he was playing those games. How many women did he know who allowed him to forget the priestly role? She would like to think she belonged to a unique band, but she doubted it.

She emerged from the subway at Christopher Street and caught her breath. Her Sunday City was ankle deep, snow still falling. There were few places as beautiful as Manhattan under new snow. Minus delivery vans, thoroughfares relatively empty.

She'd had a love affair with Manhattan since her dad helped her, at eight, up those narrow metal stairs in the double decker. The wind. The speed. Broadway opening out around her . . . she would never forget those rides. Looking around, suddenly she jumped back. A yellow cab skied around the corner on two wheels, stopping where she had been standing. She took a deep, long breath and smiled.

When she let herself into the utilitarian single at Pius, a

gull, rising like a copter in the space between the hotel and
the adjoining apartment building, decanted and fell away. For
a minute, she thought with longing of her cozy apartment on
Spring. You had to sublet, you couldn't afford it and the
house. This is fine for the occasional overnight. You won't be
doing any entertaining!

Besides the narrow bed, someone had placed a rocker facing
the eight feet between the outer walls, facing the opening over
the Hudson, facing the light, tiny portion of sky. She put the
briefcase with the last chapter of the Valery article in it, on
this, setting it rocking, lightly. Pulling off her boots, she immediately got her feet wet standing in the puddle they'd made
on the carpet. Groaning, she started for the adjoining shower,
pulling her sweater over the mass of tricolor hair, hopping out
of the green wool skirt. She had plenty of time for a long, hot
shower.

At six-fifteen, she cut across Bedford to Seventh as one of
St. Vincent's ambulances caterwauled and sloshed its way
north, snowflakes back-lit red and flashing. She had never hesitated to take on the walk to Little Italy when she was living
on Spring. In New York, what were a few blocks? This wasn't
that much farther.

But she hadn't bargained on the snow slowing her as much
as it did. At seven-fifteen she turned hurriedly south on Mulberry in order to intersect Hester, and fell. As she burst
through the door of Puglia's, she was grateful Arthur had not
suggested Patrissy with its elegant charm.

She could feel the sweat running down under both arms to
her ribs. The waiter, strolling toward her between the long,
plank tables, looked amused and then glanced around protec-
tively. Probably grateful he's placed no one near the door. She

shook herself discreetly, as a dog would coming from a swim. Motioning her to follow, the waiter turned and headed toward the next room.

Arthur Danley, standing when he saw her, shook his head in bemusement. Power. Mir felt it the first time they met. The cleric in traditional black waiting with her while the ancient toaster slowly warmed their English muffins; it never browned them. The breakfast room at Pius, full of clergy who seemed to know this and stuck to muffins.

A priest. Ho-hum. A bishop who handled himself like a green beret. Hummm. She had always been partial to men who oozed energy. He wasn't as tall as Eli or her first husband Brian.

Brian's energy leaked out in superfluous, inconsequential ways. She had been a child marrying a child who couldn't hold a job, couldn't finish a thing.

Eli, always controlled, had great strength, always contained.

Arthur. When she stood near him she felt the way she used to feel as a young girl when the Queen docked, and she went to stand on the pier at her berth under her bow. He loomed.

He loomed now in a very expensive-looking black ski jacket he had unzipped, but not removed. The waiters knew him. They'd met five times. No one ever called him Bishop or Your Reverence in her presence. It was always Sir.

Once she was seated, he bent to the waiter, "Hold the order, Sorze? I think we'd better let the lady drip." The dark, heavyset Sicilian winked in complicity She was more than a little annoyed at the two of them, but damned if she'd show it. She tried to feel coy and protected so that these 'feminine' traits would show. Danley just looked at her, grinning.

"Wine?"

"Beer." She made an effort to soften her voice. "I think I lost a bit of moisture walking over, footing was worse than I expected."

"You look as if you gained some," he nodded at the droplets hanging and sparkling in her hair.

"I look pretty bad huh?"

"You look great!" 'Great' descended into a space somewhere and sent a rill of heat flopping over and over at the tip of her spine.

She was not partial to robust skin coloring, too much like her own. Once blond, now grey, he still had very fair, slightly pink skin. His large hands were never stilled; they drummed now on the edge of the dark wood.

As she leaned back from the table, shook and patted her hair hopefully into place, she felt his eyes on her, questioning. "I must say," he said, "I was very pleased to find your message on my machine."

"You cancelled your game?"

He pursed his lips, nodding. "Poker I can play any Sunday."

"I think you're playing this Sunday." Startled, he looked at her, then threw back his head and laughed.

She laughed along with him. Then, apologetically, "It was a spur of the moment decision. I wasn't coming down until the morning."

"Coming from where?"

"My old home. I gave up my apartment and moved back up to Westchester. I've decided I'm a writer first and foremost. I can't get what I'd like to do, done, down here. I've kept three days of proofreading at Linters and am finishing a freelance piece on Paul Valery."

"Humph." The grunt expressed a measure of respect.

"I know you appreciate Valery. Not everyone does you know."

He nodded. "Clergy and medical people do."

"The elite?"

"Not necessarily. What made you call?"

He was no fool. He looked coolly across at her. His fingers were still. The breadth of his shoulders filled the space that the three Asian men across the way could only fill together.

"I'm very hungry."

He lowered his eyes. It could wait 'til later. He raised the waiter for their order with a bare look.

The first English muffin meeting with Arthur Danley had been—as far as she was concerned—innocence itself. After all, the place had been crawling with Roman collars. She had been acutely aware of her hair, all over the place, and the simple neat coif of the sister waiting on the group of prelates at the nearby table. The friend who had borrowed her apartment for a steamy afternoon alliance had not given the requisite signal that they were through. Someone at the office suggested Pius House, neglecting to say it was a Catholic hospice.

Sleepy, having the first coffee of her day, Mir found being surrounded by men supposedly off limits gave her indigestion. She acutely remembered making her way across the endless reaches in her usual lope, past the black garbed figures making discreet conversation, an English muffin in hand, and the devil in her saying, jump, fly, waltz! All kinds of anti-Pharisee indignation surfaced when she was near religious. It was awful.

She was busy swearing to herself she would never eat there again when a powerful presence turned up at her shoulder and grinned. Danley had shown her his English muffin with a look that said, I know, funny isn't it? There was a twinkle in his blue eyes while he acted as the perfect exemplar of obeisance before all Mary models, all mothers, all woman-fold.

They were on stage and when they finally retrieved their slightly toasted muffins, she would not have been at all surprised to hear a smattering of applause.

Back at her table, she looked down at the buttered English and wondered what she could do to make it palatable. She ended up eating it under an inch of grape jelly. Even then, she had to get up for a refill on the coffee to swallow it.

Finishing, looking neither right or left, she let herself out of the cafeteria-like room and bolted up three flights of stairs. So much for that!

A month later, she ran into him at the Nicholas Roerich exhibit. He recognized her right away, he said. She, engrossed in the deep ceruleans, pale lavenders and mauves surrounding Kanchenjunga, refused to break concentration—anymore than she already had—to look directly at the individual who was intentionally, she was sure of it, invading her space. So hulking sure they belonged to the earth! The way many men crowd you made her furious. Pretending she was unaware of it, she slid with eyes unlifted over to the Little Tibet Mongolian painting Roerich did between 1923 and 1927. He titled it "Tidings of the Eagle."

She had almost convinced herself that the impertinent viewer was no longer there when she heard the words, "Do you only talk with strange men over breakfast?" She looked up then, startled, and flushed red to the roots, remembering.

He didn't have the collar turned on the beautifully cut charcoal grey pinstripe. Another man hovered in the next room, evidently his chauffeur. He went over and dismissed him after they had gone thoroughly through the museum for almost two hours, painting by painting. She thought it would have been kind of him to let the man go before that, but that wasn't the way it happened.

He called her for lunch a week after with tickets for the Georgia O'Keeffe exhibit.

She never saw the Roman collar again.

He introduced himself as Arthur Danley. It was the slight Asian man in the black uniform that tipped her. He had called him, "Your Reverence, Bishop Danley." She had the feeling the man said it loud enough for her to hear clearly, even though she stood across the room from them.

"Who looks to the sky before lowering their pants? I mean, he was despicable! There he sat on the big lower limb of the old maple, right over a posted sign. Never let on he was there. Didn't see him until I got up to leave." Arthur Danley laughed so loud the three Asian men across the way all looked in unison at their table. "You wouldn't have done it? You *would* have done it! You would have done just the very same thing, I can see it on your face. Men!"

"How about Caffe Bondo? I could do with some very good espresso and pastry." He licked his lips. He was still chuckling when Sorze returned with change. He helped her on with her coat and when the two of them reached the street, he tucked her hand into his pocket and with an arm about her waist, started high-stepping it through the snow along Hester toward Mulberry.

Chapter Nine

He glimpsed a sashay of pink lack curtains against the glass of the first floor apartment as he turned the car in through the driveway's unbroken snow. By the time he parked, Mrs. Poole, wearing barn boots and a parka three sizes too big—probably her late husbands—was at the side entrance, taking bites from the rounded slope obscuring his steps with her aluminum, non-stick surface shovel.

"Terrible unreliable they all are, Mr. Janah, don't respect honest work. Young people today, don't know." The lowest step appeared. "That Greelie boy said he would be here soon as snow. Soon as snow, he said, big laugh that was. Pay 'im good . . . don't respect money either." The second step appeared.

"Mrs. Poole, I'll be back down as soon as I change, I'll do that for you."

"Can't have you doing that, Mr. Janah, you work hard 'n' all . . . ain't right" . . . but the escaped sigh as she leaned against the outer door frame, told him that was exactly what she had been hoping for.

The second floor landing was quiet. He took the remainder of the stairs in twos, switched on the light within his own place, walked through to the bedroom to return within moments wearing old jeans, a battered wool ski jacket that had belonged to one of the boys, and a black knit hat. Pulling his old boots on by the door, he grabbed up gloves and bolted downstairs.

"Truly, I'm happy to do it . . . been sitting too much today." He shooed the old woman gently back into her apartment and proceeded to cut a straight path out to the street.

There was very little traffic and the hush that fell with the white stuff gave him the feeling of being deep within one of those bubbles you play with as a child. He was the tiny toy man shovelling the walks along the sleepy street. Someone up-ended his bubble periodically and he all but disappeared in the gusting snow.

He found his thoughts returning to Father Elias. The priest's ease and inner peacefulness was more striking than anything he said. Very few men at his age, he figured forty-four or five, exude peace. Did he find life engrossing? Rewarding? A challenge? All of them? None?

The word completion came to mind. He dwelt on it, rolling it around like a licorice drop. It surprised him. Snow flew to the gutter as he swung great arcs, enjoying the play of his shoulder muscles, the torque of his spine. The no-parking in effect allowed him to wall it for the plow.

He was surprised because he viewed Father Elias' life as narrow and circumscribed . . . as he had the Hebrew equivalent years ago. Strangely, the priest seemed content . . . not only content, he appeared right with his world. Takes all kinds I guess. He shook his head and a white cascade fell from his hat to his brows. From there it sifted to his lashes, he blinked clear, came to the end of the walk, turned and widened the path back against the flower garden that, come summer, would be alive with purple nasturtiums and blue phlox, Mrs. P's favorite colors.

While he replaced the shovel, the door to his landlady's apartment opened. Her sight might be failing, but there was nothing wrong with her hearing. "I know I wouldn't be able to get you to sit down for this." She held a tiny mug on a flowered saucer out to him, steam rising through a froth of cream on the surface of the liquid. He stomped his feet free of snow, removed his gloves, smiling at her and took the delicate china in hand.

"Glad we got it done tonight," he gestured back over his shoulder, "it would have been very heavy in the morning! I'll check before going to work, take care of whatever accumulation we get during the night. That will give you tomorrow to find out what happened to Andy."

"Thank you!" She seemed very frail standing beside her high, dark door in the light falling on the landing. When he drained the tiny mug, she gave a sigh of contentment.

Back in his own apartment, while waiting for the kettle to boil for coffee—he couldn't remember when he last drank cocoa—he called information for Mir's number. There was no listing.

"No," the operator said somewhat crossly, "it is not unlisted, it isn't a number, period!"

How like her he thought, she still hasn't gotten around to having her phone connected. He was restless. He thought of calling Marion and hesitated; he had deliberately not thought of the time they spent together the other day. Something he hadn't known about himself had surfaced, a matter that made him more restless . . . he needed time.

Flicking the kettle off again, he opened the door into the coolness of the practice room and turned on the light. Stripping off his shirts and jeans, he pulled on a pair of black sweat pants that had been hanging behind the door. Naked torso, bare feet, he stood with the South behind him facing the North star.

Think of water, he commanded, gazing on the smooth vanished wood ten feet away. Instead of water, angry red buttocks and the flush and excitement of humiliation came to him.

He concentrated on allowing the chi to drop below his navel to the place of roil and turbulence. He instructed his shoulders to relax, his arms to be loose.

With concentration there is stillness. There was no stillness. None of the five essential qualities were present tonight. He did the only other thing he could, he began Tai Chi Chuan as a whirling dervish.

He focused on being true to the movements, without clarity, balance, lightness, or slowness and minus all calm. Rapidly, he moved from 'grasp the bird's tail' to 'ward off left.' Immediately he was 'warding off right,' 'rolling back.'

'Single whip' set off sparks within his lumbar region. 'Shoulder strike' . . . 'stork spreads wings' . . . he concentrated on fidelity and speed. Keeping the movements from slowing, he synchronized tempo to chaos.

Physical certainty filled him at the first 'apparent closure.' 'Carrying tiger to mountain' . . . mind obliterated emotion . . . mind protecting body from destroying itself. In the partnership of body and mind, he'd always know the heart of matter was mind.

Tai Chi was first and foremost a mind exercise. By the time he reached 'snake creeps down,' he had to force himself to keep up the fast tempo. Every cell of his body was crying for slowness and calmness. He ignored them.

At 'fair lady works shuttles,' the energy sank low. The gold snake stretching, uncoiling, began to wake.

A brilliance of physical certainty 'kicked horizontal' 'bent bow and shot the tiger.' Body at play, mind at east. The pivot of Tao, ego and non-ego no longer exposed.

Sinking into 'apparent closure,' a word came to him. Hsin, the Chinese word for heart and mind . . . which cannot be separated. Calm mind directing, method refines. Subtle, profound, practical mind directs body with increasing perfection. And the very certainty rebounds to increasing mental ease and equilibrium.

Taking a deep breath, he dropped into beginning stance again. This time the way it should be . . .

Later, sitting with coffee and a shot of cognac, reading the *Times* article by Benedict Nightingale on the Irish actor Ray McAnally, he was caught up by the rightness of the actor's words. "The body is limited, but the mind is infinite." Just as McAnally knew he could play any part in the world mentally, Eli knew it was possible for mind to direct body through all one hundred and twenty eight movements of Tai Chi . . . even though the body were paralyzed, insensate, confined to a wheelchair.

Lost in thought, he put the Arts and Leisure section down. Ray McAnally's words were the realest thing he'd heard that day: "The body is altered, physically and chemically altered by the mind."

One wakes eventually, but deep snow deactivates one's usual leverage. It is hard then for the mind to take up the play of the game. Very slowly, Mir turned in the bed to gauge the light. Against the wall of the building opposite, an oblique triangular patch of it, told her it was almost seven a.m. It did not matter that she had never stayed in this particular room before. The snow had stopped. The light from the East was low.

Coffee! It would be an hour before the cafeteria downstairs opened. She thought of the patisserie on the way to the office . . . fresh croissants . . . large mugs . . .

As she lathered under the shower spray, presenting her foamy torso to the pelting warmth, she thought of Arthur Danley. He had a great zest for life; she'd had a thoroughly good time last night.

Curious though. She was sure he had known what her intended next article was before she broached the subject. But he didn't give her an answer. He looked at her as if he were assessing a trotter at Yonkers. When he finally spoke, he referred to the fact that she was staying in town because of the weather and would she have dinner with him again tomorrow.

That is, today. He was picking her up at ten to six. Dinner at Porto Bello, a little cucina Italiana, he said. He had a great appetite for Italian. She sucked her belly in and patted its slight oval. She was going to gain weight knowing this man.

Did she enjoy Les Paul? Yes, then it was settled; they would burn off the calories walking to Fat Tuesdays on Third and Seventeenth to hear him. A man who could not give her a simple yes or no was surely being quite purposeful in other matters.

He had been quite purposeful when he said No! to CBGB's. Looking somewhat startled, he asked her what on earth she wanted to go to a place 'like that' for? Bowery and Bleecker was definitely off limits. She wondered why; he certainly could handle himself.

Somewhat annoyed at this paternalistic attitude, she had opened her mouth. Maybe a little hardcore in spots, but not exactly in line with the male dancers with their boxer shorts down around their ankles in the burlesque theaters on Times Square. It had been a long time since her father told her what he thought was appropriate work for women. But time had not dissipated the hot angry sting.

She thrust that at Danley and was rewarded by a flush that started in his lower neck and rose to his ears. His response to the all-male revues differed from the former. One was merely scuzzy and uncomfortably off-limits. One was unmentionable. She smiled to herself remembering the cigar smoking maleness of him . . . the ease with which he lifted her over the snow banks . . . the evident pleasure he took in holding her far longer than he needed to.

At ten to nine she pushed open the office door. "Mrs. Janah! Oh, Mrs. Janah!" Cornelius Weber, one of her bosses, was wringing his hands just inside the opening. She had the feeling he had been pacing back and forth between the water cooler, the clock, and the door. "Mrs. Janah, such terrible weather!" She nodded, waiting, he had not called her Mrs. Janah passionately three times because of the weather. "So unfortunate. Traffic so devastatingly snarled. Oh, I do believe these things are arranged to test me. Why must it happen today?"

Flushed and exhilarated from her walk, she tried to look concerned for this most friable of the partners who to her mind, was always being tested. "Lawrence is ill. He was supposed to meet her," a small sob escaped his throat, his hand did a so-so wobble in mid air as if his partner in a glider was encountering air currents.

Barbara Latouche, author of *Bedevil Alphonse* was arriving at Port Authority at ten that morning. The poor woman simply detested trains. She would not fly; flying was abhorrent to her. And most importantly, she had been assured that someone would meet her bus, and she was terrified of large cities. Mir, listening to this spiel, wondered what the creature was made of.

She had given a sympathetic grunt which he in his anxiety had taken for some kind of marvelous windfall. "You agree? Oh! I am so relieved. Someone must be there to meet her," pump . . . pump . . . "thank you!" His slender fingers grasping the end of her mitten, nearly shook it off.

The elevator operator taking her off in the opposite direction from the flow of traffic, glanced her way, "Short day huh?" On the street, she struck off again, this time Northwest. Two young women were helping each other from a taxi whose rear wheels were stuck in a snow bank. The smell of rubber burns came to her along with the shrill cry of the wheels.

Port Authority, amazingly vacant, looked as if half the arriving buses hadn't made it. She was twenty minutes early, so veered to the ladies' room on the central plaza. A breathing spell . . . the kind of time she utilized for all sorts of things. She pulled a squat, plastic bottle of Listerine from her pocketbook and took a large mouthful.

Sitting in the cubicle, she sloshed the liquid back and forth therapeutically against her ageing gums. Paltry little proofreading this morning, my dear. There were some shuffling footsteps on the other side of the stall. She listened, but heard no voices.

Flushing, she gathered herself together, and stepped out into a ring of silent girls. "Madam will need towels, show her the cleanest sink, Viv. And soap! Of course, Tina, Madam will need soap. Soap is expensive these days, isn't it girls?" There was a murmur of assent.

She stood silently, as one after another of the six haphazard citizens touched her arm. The circle drew together. But this was all too silly, she thought. None of them was over sixteen. Straggly hair, oversized army jackets, pinched faces . . . without looking any one in the face, she felt the undercurrent energy.

"Now watch the puddle, Madam," the leader had taken her arm and was trying to steer her around the overflow from a nearby cubicle. "We aim to please, don't we, girls?"

Listerine suds started trickling down her throat. With her free hand she pointed toward her puffy cheeks, coughed, squashed an urge to vomit, and lunged; the circle opened, six pair of irregularly clad feet backed away as she broke for the sink. She ran the water; when she looked up from rinsing her mouth, she was alone.

She looked around the derelict squalor of the restroom, why did they run? It could be a dream. The blocked plumbing. The wet floor. The dirt. The lack of towels. Six street girls playing at BIG bad energy.

"I struck out twice. The first woman I approached, looked at me as if I were crazed, changed her suitcase rapidly to her outer hand and hurried away. When the second woman laughed in my face, I decided to hang back, process of elimination, you know."

Mir laughed long and soft, remembering. "Finally, there was no one left but this wispy, little grey-haired lady, clutching her bag with both hands, darting furtive glances left and right. I swear I couldn't say it. I could not go up and ask *her* if she was Roxanne LaTouche."

"What happened?" Arthur Danley's eyes were full of humor.

"She came to me, one half-step at a time. She edged forward, clutching the bag like a shield." Mir pitched her voice high, "'My dear, you wouldn't happen to know a Mr. Weber at Linten's Publishing Company?' 'Roxanne' I asked. Couldn't get out the second half. Her friends came up with the nom de plume. *No* one would suspect her of writing those steamy novels."

"Someday I must show you the catacombs under old St. Pat's. You enjoy oddities. There was a time the Church was into temporal power."

"When has it not?"

He grimaced, pursing his full lips. "They stopped hiding their wealth in subterranean caverns in 1913 . . ."

"What about the art treasures moldering away under Rome?"

"Ornery tonight, aren't we?" But he conceded with a nod of bushy, grey hair. She suddenly had a picture of him bending his mitered head to strike the blow that confirmed you a soldier of Christ. A soldier's soldier.

"I've read that some felt His Holiness wanted to reside in the United States back when the original St. Patrick's was built."

"Some very angry people fought what they did not know. Those catacombs came in handy more than once."

"I would like to see them. What's under new St. Pat's?" He hunched his shoulders, looked at his wine. Mir knew he would not answer. She felt incorrigible. "They knock them off? The builders? Bury them in the tower supports so they wouldn't talk? Not a good idea to let too many know what's under the ground . . . when you hope to wield power . . ."

He was shaking his head back and forth as if arguing with himself. There was a smile playing around the corner of his generous mouth. She decided to chance it.

"Am I doing the article on the Monastery of the Annunciation?"

"No one can stop you."

"Do I have your support?" She waited.

"Yes." Clipped, it dropped like a pebble in a goldfish bowl. A tiny spume of dust rose from the bottom.

"You don't like the idea."

He sighed. "In some ways I think you'll be more trouble than you're worth." That gave her cause to nod assent.

"You will help me though, keep my facts straight?"

He rubbed a finger pensively through a brow . . . pushing the brush up, letting it fall, pushing it up, letting it fall. "Keep tabs?"

"Something like that."

"If you insist." But he had already thought it out and decided there were advantages.

"I appreciate it."

He frowned, shaking his head. "Don't thank me yet."

Chapter Ten

Mind is the knower; mind is the object known. There was the brightness of linen everywhere. Damian, dropping a fold softly so it would not crease, laid the tunic in the drawer atop the green brocade of the chasuble. Sacristy light drenched the mounded snow. Through the large window looking into the garden, the yew, unusually tall, gave a little lurch against the glass, settling new fur about its shoulders.

Always the loosed delight. Silence—the snow.

The bells in the tower muffled the call to Mass. She heard a step on the other side of the wall.

Sister sacristan was always released from silence to speak with the officiating priest, but Father Elias never spoke until after Mass. If he needed something, a note was passed through the drawer, a tap on wood advising of its arrival.

Placing the matching stole, she folded the white linen cloth for the handwashing, laying it on a diagonal just across the edge of the green outer garment. So much white tended to forsake boundaries. They were such silly inconspicuous little things, utterly unabsorbent, always getting lost.

He sounded in good spirits. Truly, the man had done an

about face in the last few years. There had been talk of an imminent nervous breakdown when he first arrived. Those times he came with Monsignor Reilly you could feel the tension, gloom, and nervous energy. Reilly kept muttering, "give 'im time."

Well, time it was then that healed all wounds—and prayer. They might mother the whole Asian peoples, but she would always direct the main thrust of her prayer toward the priests.

She waited while he removed the vestments in the order in which they were put on, first the tunic, then the stole and the chasuble. Waiting to see there was nothing else needed, she then let herself noiselessly out of the sacristy into the muted light of the enclosed wing of the church.

"How do you feel about grabbing some real breakfast . . . pancakes, sausage, bacon . . . ?" Eli, still wearing the torn ski jacket and knit hat looked hopefully at Walt Bathesday and John Fay who had their coats on before he said 'bacon.' They stood grinning like two kids on reprieve from school.

Fay jerked his chin. "You paying?"

"Yeah, let's go. I need something to stick to my ribs this morning." Eli led the way.

Bath plucked at the old ski jacket as he passed, "Bit casual this morning, aren't we?"

Eli just shook his head in exasperation. "Damn plows. I think they deliberately shove their load in any poor fart's opening."

They wisely refrained from comment.

"By the way, bring what you've gathered so far." Bath patted his overcoat pocket. Fay tapped his fist against the spines of the spiral notebook tucked in the breast pocket of his suit jacket.

Mom Molinari, in her beaming bulk, soon had them surrounded with steaming plates and fraternal smells. She was in her element; three hungry men! There was no talk for twenty minutes.

Then Eli gave a great sigh and leaned back, "God, I needed that, feel like I've been up for hours."

Bath wiped his mouth. "Well, I haven't been up all that long, but it sure was good." Fay agreed, swiping his plate one last time with a hunk of sweet roll. "Why don't I start?" Bath said. They watched as he dug deep into the overcoat he'd draped over the back of his chair.

"Father Arturo Polaski. Thirty-four years old. Diocesan priest. His folks still live in the Bay area where he grew up. Sheepshead Bay area. Honor student all the way. Secretary and all around gofer for his excellency Bishop Danley. Studious, sensitive, well-read. The man speaks five languages." They could tell that Bath was impressed. "He speaks Chinese, a southern dialect spoken in the vicinity of the Sung-shan mountains in Honan province. That's one of China's sacred mountains, the central sacred one. There are sacred mountains in their North, South, East, and West."

Eli, fascinated, was considering this new facet of Walt Bathesday. He grinned. "Do you have the mountains' names too?"

Bath, realizing his leg was being pulled, flushed a little. "Well, I got kinda interested in it all. They make pilgrimages to these mountains. The pilgrimages may take any form or shape as long as the individual knows it's the one he should be making."

"Or she," John Fay interjected.

"Yeah. Whatever." Brusquely . . . "Didn't mean to get sidetracked. Father Polaski also speaks Vietnamese and Cambodian. The Cambodian dialect is one spoken in the Cardamom Mountain area near Battambang."

Fay raised his head. "Another sacred mountain?"

Bath did not deign a reply. "Father Arturo Polaski also speaks Spanish. For a couple of years now, he's been doing sanctuary work with the Nicaraguans. Danley, I hear, gave him the green light there.

"Then, I had some time left, so I took Mrs. Henry. No big deal," he sloughed off Fay's thanks. "Mrs. Henry lives over on Eighth Street within walking distance of the monastery. Fifty-seven years old, mother of four (who've all left home), she lives with her husband. He works for the phone company. Pleasant middle-aged woman, likes to keep busy. Once in a while she cleans for other people, but she always cleans the extern quarters and the church for the sisters. She was cleaning that Tuesday, but she had to leave early for a doctor's appointment, so she missed our little delivery. I checked. She *did* have a doctors's appointment. A matter of cancer her husband doesn't know about . . . yet.

"Five ladies help her out, altar society or something. Flowers, decorations for feast days, that kind of stuff . . . but she insists on doing all the cleaning herself." Bath stopped for a moment and looked at them. "Mr. and Mrs. Henry lost a son in the Cambodian conflict. From what I hear, she accepts it as the will of God. Her husband on the other hand, has some rough things to say. Phone company's not the great twenty-first century integrated ideal . . . so he's not exactly on the spot." He looked first at one, then the other. "Says he'd rather

111

kill the gooks than work with them, if it comes to that. He has ten years before retirement."

Walt Bathesday cocked an eyebrow while he flipped his pad. "The good bishop. Fifty-nine years old, native New Yorker, Hayes High School."

Eli smiled. "Went right into the seminary after graduation?"

"No." Bath sucked saliva through his teeth. "He joined the Marines. Tough street punk from what I hear. An old teacher of his resides in the Upstate Home for Senior Priests. He remembers Blackbeard Danley, says he had red hair, but they called him Blackbeard." Bath gave Eli a quizzical shrug.

"Superiors in the service thought Danley was going to make a life of it," Bath continued. "Thirty years, and they remember him still. Say he had the makings of a great soldier. Three four-year tours . . . hand picked for Special Forces . . . Sent to Nam from Korea. When the powers that be did not want to, or could not bring themselves to, use guerilla tactics, he disappeared behind the scenes somewhere. Everyone's hazy on just where Operational Assistant Danley went.

"He surprised them by asking for release at the end of his third tour to join the seminary of all things. You're looking at cardinal material now.

"Religious conversion?" Bath pursed his lips. "Don't know. Happens. Gad, thirty years is a long time to remember; some of these coots were *real* old!" He shook his head in disbelief.

John Fay's contented face had long since waved good-bye to his plate when he felt Eli's eyes on him. He cleared his throat. "The kid, Del Martin, cute little twerp. Asked if I wanted to trade playing cards with him. Do I look *that* young?"

Bath leaned forward, "Hey, I didn't think kids did that anymore."

Fay looked at him incredulously. He began again. "Del is eleven. Lives with his family just over the line into Incarnation parish. They used to live on Fifth. His dad misses his bagels."

Eli interrupted, "Where do you get good bagels around here?"

"Breadstuffs."

"Breadstuffs from Annunciation to Incarnation . . . bagels from Breadstuffs Bakery to Mr. Martin." Eli grinned at his own witticism.

"Del is real pleased with himself, pockets three dollars a week, a veritable budding capitalist. He figured the route out all by himself. Teachers' conference that afternoon . . . half day . . . he arrived at the monastery about one p.m. Didn't see anything. Wishes he'd gone for the bagels first. Sure wishes he'd seen those hands and feet."

"Bloodthirsty little goblin."

"Naw. All male kids are like that.

"Father William Strisbel," Fay continued, "mid-forties. Kinda your average activist. Has been warned to cool it. Been in jail twice for pouring blood on Selective Service files. Diocesan." This last came out with a perplexed grunt that said in John Fay's experience only Jesuits poured blood. "Danley sent him to St. Hilary's. Been there two years now. Parishioners like him. Does more than his share of work, no complaints. Doesn't seem to harbor antipathy, anti-Asian that is. Quiet guy, writes poetry on the side."

Fay flipped his pad. "Father Jeff Allen seems very close to Father Stephen Elias. Same size, same build." Walt did a

Groucho imitation with his left eyebrow. "No, not like that at all, like brothers. They get along real well; everyone says so."

Eli interjected, "Father Allen is the one who takes over Father Elias' work when he's out of town."

"Allen is thirty-five," Fay said, referring to his notes. "Long Island kid, large family. Real sports freak. Coaches the boys' basketball, soccer, and baseball." He counted them off on his fingers. "Kids at the elementary school say he's good."

"How tall is Father Strisbel?" Eli asked.

"About five eight." Eli wrote it down in his notebook. "Cheery guy, sure can't see him dashing around with freezer bags of cow's blood. Never know, though."

Eli nodded. "You've been thorough, both of you." He raised a finger for more coffee.

John Fay stood for a moment, turned his chair around and sat down, straddling it. When Sebastian Molinari had gone back to the counter with the coffee pot, he resumed talking. "Father Stephen Elias, fifty-one years old, Diocesan priest, another native New Yorker. Been at St. Hilary's fifteen years now. A flake, I'm afraid. A loser. Barely made it through seminary. It was St. Hilary's or the loony bin for priests." He enjoyed the curious looks of the other two. "Sorry, but he was in a bad way. From all I hear, nerves completely shot. A pacifist at one time. Marched. Demonstrated. Never had the guts to sprinkle the blood of the lamb on the doorposts . . ." His voice trailed off.

The old monsignor, O'Reilly it was, asked to have him sent to St. Hilary's. Thought he could help him. Guess he thought he was having some sort of vocational crisis. Seems to have worked; he's found his non-threatening niche. Parishioners say he's easy to get along with. Really enjoys servicing the monastery."

A blast of air escaped forcefully from Bath, who then pounded the table, "Haw, haw, haw . . . the bull on demand huh?"

John Fay looked at his partner in disgust before continuing. "Oh, yeah, he was a twin. Not identical. But old teachers say it was hard to tell the brothers apart, on the surface, that is. There the resemblance ended. Father Elias had a brother who was darn good at everything . . . girls, sports, grades . . ." Eli took note of the order. "Stephen Elias was not too good with women." From the expression on his face they could tell that the cleric had been a perfect dolt, as far as John Fay was concerned. "He couldn't graze a football held eight inches from his toe. And he failed, failed, failed.

"He studied medicine, barely made the internship, then flunked out. He ended up joining the priesthood. At about the same time, his brother de-railed a proposed law career to join the Marines as a fighter pilot in Nam. He crashed his Phantom II. Some feel that Father Elias' breakdown, if not caused by, was at the very least exacerbated by his brother's disappearance and death.

"That old Monsignor O'Reilly must have been quite the devil on wheels from what I heard, ran the rectory like boot camp. Evidently helped Elias." Fay's eyebrows were quizzical. "Haven't met the Father, from all I hear he's no longer slated for the loony bin." Eli, musing to himself, was noncommittal. The person Fay was describing and the man he had spoken with did not seem like one and the same. Curious.

By late afternoon, Bath and Fay, caught up on their paperwork, were on their way back to the neighborhood of middle-class homes abutting the Annunciation, in hopes of catching certain individuals home. Eli spent nearly an hour with the lieutenant sketching in the investigation. Answering Morley's questions took longer than he had expected. The lieutenant didn't cite the pressures he was under, but Eli knew they were still there; Morley was too thorough. And he was complimentary. He was only openly appreciative when he agreed with what you were doing and when he wanted to make you feel easy and clear about the job you were on so you could do even better.

Eli hadn't changed from the old work clothes. They gave him a devil-may-care attitude he thought, catching sight of himself leaving the office at the end of the hall.

The temperature had risen abruptly into the low thirties. Rain pelted the accumulated snow, glazing the surface. A glare of ice formed on all the cleared thoroughfares. It was going to be slosh, slosh, slide, slosh for a while. He decided to call Marion.

She was pleased, her voice was light. "Well, I'm playing homebody today. I thought I was coming down with a cold, so I decided to cook myself chicken stew and dumplings." She took a deep sniff. "Smells great. If you're not afraid of germs and you're not fussy, you're welcome. I'm working on a blueberry pie, the blueberries are big as thumbnails. I got them at the market before the snow hit. They're really beautiful. I wonder where they came from." Her voice deepened. "I'd like company."

She must have run to buzz the door open with her hands covered with flour. The wall was smudged white; a trail of powder led into the kitchen. Eli followed. It was a modern apartment, very pleasant, very bright. She had accentuated the kitchens' single saffron wall with bright red pots and pans which hung in helter-skelter angular fashion from an overhead rack. Below this, not quite in the center of the floor but close to one counter, a large chop block stood on squat red legs.

She turned from the wooden chop block to wave him in, a streak of white across her forehead. Gesturing to a cabinet over the sink she said, "Help yourself to a drink." She turned back, then stretched full across the surface of the block—rounding the paisley print of her skirt so that thousands of geometric swirls loomed loud and clear—and uncurled a pie crust from the roller in her hand onto the counter where there was room for it to lie unbroken.

She wore a soft white knit top with a low scoop neck. A tiny white apron protected the front of the magenta skirt, inadequately. Her hair in damp tendrils at the base of her neck was almost the same color as the tail feathers of the cockatoo in the cage by the window. The crested parrot started talking wildly when Eli came up behind her and put his arms about her waist.

He intended to kiss her on the neck and go and make himself a drink. She was mixing flour and sugar with her hands in a big aluminum bowl full of deep purple, almost black, blueberries.

Intentions. Intentions. He watched himself slide the sweep of paisley slowly up over the dimpled backs of her knees . . . up the rounded thighs.

"No! Eli . . . my pie . . . let me finish the pie!"

The material inched up over her bare bottom, "Just checking." His hands smoothed the firm flesh; it was silky and pink. There were no straps, no strap marks. Before she knew what was happening, he lifted her, bent her over, and spread her wide.

She fought him, her voice this time angry, very angry. In the scuffle that followed, the bowl under her breasts tipped over, emptied, rolling off the chop block falling clattering on the kitchen tile, scattering blue balls.

The bird jumped about crazily in its cage making tch-tch . . . tch-tch sounds. Keeping her pinned, he sucked saliva into the front of his mouth, collecting it on his tongue. Then picking her up to his face, he let all of the liquid pour out of his mouth onto her asshole. Gently . . . oh so gently . . . he started licking around and around, up and down. She went limp under his hands, a low guttural sound coming from deep within her. There was the taste of spices. Her whole back arched.

Dropping his right hand away from her buttock then, he unzipped his fly, literally popping out of the welcome opening, he brought her wet pussy down on the erect, hot rod cradled in his hand, putting it exactly where he knew she wanted it. Her elbows hit the chop block squirting blue back at him from either side.

He humped so hard her breasts flew out of the knit top. First one, then the other, they fell in the blueberries where they ground back and forth until there was a purple mash on the surface of the table. The pink nipples reflecting in the shine of the broiler across the way, grew darker and darker.

With his left hand, his whole body supporting her while she withdrew her arms, he drew the sweater down to her waist to give her more freedom to move. Seemingly oblivious of everything but what lay between, she flexed and rolled back and forth. Smooth, Frictionless. Blueberries squashed under her breasts, under his hands, under his penis, in the cleft of her body. Little rivulets of blue ran along each of her arms.

She looked like she was wearing blue war paint. Every part of her was streaked except her bottom. He turned her over and sat her down squarely on the fruit pulp, while kissing her on the mouth long and hard. Her breasts were sticky and there were blueberry stains on her chin. Laying her gently back on the table, he drew her naked buttocks forward, doctor-like to the edge of it, then lay her legs, one after the other, up against his chest.

She swore later that he stuffed her with blueberries, that there were blueberries falling from her vagina the rest of the night.

They took a bath in lieu of pie and cleaned blueberries from her ass, laughing. That started it up all over again in the jacuzzi.

"Janah, we have to stop this."

"Why?"

Late that night, Eliaphus D. Janah let himself into his apartment, walked unerringly in the dark to the swollen armchair and dropped. He sat there for about twenty minutes. Then he got up, put on a light, looked at his watch, and dialed Walt Bathesday's number.

"Walt, sorry, I know it's late." Bath didn't sound as if he had been asleep. "Can you find out how many times Polaski's been overseas? Southeast Asia for a start. Oh, I would think with his background he would be able to travel anywhere over there. I'd also like the computer printout on Danley's overseas travel for ten years. No, go back farther on Danley. While

119

you're dealing with passports and visas, check Strisbel and Allen. Yeah, they're quite an interesting group. I'm curious about the old Monsignor's routes . . . got a feeling it started with him. Not sure yet.

"What do you really think about Arthur Danley dropping the service all those years ago . . . his religious conversion?" He listened to Bath. "But we always fight the old war, so what's new? They couldn't see it wasn't going to work in Nam. The Marines told them. Special Forces told them." There was a stream of crisp, salient expletives from the man on the other end.

"Hell, I can see the bitterness . . . watching the stupidity of it all . . . yeah." There was a long silence between them.

"Walt, imagine you're a street-wise punk who's found his nook, his hole, his corner of the world . . . you're in a situation like Danley's . . . what do you do? You join the Church?" He nodded. "That's what I thought."

They talked for about ten more minutes. Then Eli asked, "One last thing, could I have the names of the rest of the sacred mountains? No, I'm not kidding."

On the pad of paper by the phone he wrote: East—Tai-shan in Shantung. South—Heng-shan in Hunan. West—Hua-shan in Shensi. North—Heng-shan in Hopei. The spelling of the Northern and Southern mountains appears identical to us, but the Chinese characters are entirely different.

He thanked Bathesday, hung up and wrote the one he already knew at the end of the list . . . Central—Sung-shan in Honan.

Chapter Eleven

The vest was a reddish-brown in color. She picked it up wondering, bay or chestnut? Wondering also if the people who sewed them in the reputable little dress factory knew where they were going, the vests. Almost certainly the people did not know where they themselves were going. Such confusion among us all she thought.

Sister Damian of Mary stood in her cell at the top of the house, fresh from the allowed weekly bath. Her hair, short and wet, clung to her head. Most of her length was from the waist down. Strong haunches, her father had once remarked before mother cut him off. She patted her naked thighs. It had been years since she raced around the paths in the enclosure garden for the sheer joy of moving fast, but she felt she could still cover them in less than three minutes.

Hurriedly, for the room was none too warm, she threw the opening of the hair shirt over her head, pulled it down on her warm, still slightly moist, breasts and back, and tied the loops apron-like, at the sides. She then drew the heavy, unbleached wool undergarment, cut like a tunic, on over it.

Immediately, the flesh protested. Pricks by the hundreds bit into her soft skin. After three days, one did not feel it as much, but coming straight from the bath, skin revved up, pores open, ultra-sensitive and softened, the hair shirts were very hard to take. Their shorter cousins, the cinch-belts, were like fire ants eating into your waist. Reverend Mother Michaels did not like any one wearing either of them—or the different types of arm bands and metal chain bracelets—for more than a week at a time. She preferred three days. Damian chose those three following bath-day.

She would wear it longer right now if Michaels would only relent . . . especially now . . . living with this foreboding, this awful waiting for the thing to out.

A gust of wind blew on her from the dormer that had never been fitted for a storm window. She gave a little gasp and grabbed up the heavy wool habit. Each movement dug the short cropped horse hairs into her soft skin. A pain shot through her right breast to her back as a rigid hair slid up one of the ducts in the nipple.

Nothing forced attention like pain and discomfort. She was missing something. There was something right before her eyes that she did not see for the simple reason that she did not want to. She needed all the attention she could muster.

Damian thought back to that awful Tuesday. Again, she felt the reality of the man, the delivery, causing the turn to wobble, as one after another remnants from human bodies were placed down.

There had been a sensitiveness in the placing . . . a trust. The more she thought, the more she was sure, he *had* said, 'Poor you.' Did he know her? Was the statement one of those blanket statements that would have covered all the nuns, the monastery in general? She had a feeling he knew her.

But it was ridiculous of Detective Janah to infer it may have been Father Elias. Anyway, he never rang, he had a key. He always used his key. Was she sure it was *not* Father? Janah had asked her three times.

Sister Damian pulled the white linen toque on over her head fastening it to her shoulders with the two pins. Wrapping the stiff white band about her forehead, she looped it at the back of her skull before donning the black linen veil.

A warmth grew in her torso, mostly from the scratchy friction of the vest. When she took the shirts off, her skin was excoriated and inflamed. There had been a time when mirrors were not allowed within the monastery. She still did not have one in her cell since she did not set her hair as some of the nuns now did. She didn't need a mirror to tell her what horsehair did to your skin. All she had to do was glance down at her chest and belly. When summer heat descended, Michaels was adamant. No extra penances; heat rash was enough.

That delivery . . . she kept returning to the delivery as a trust. Stop calling it a delivery! Someone had taken an assault rifle to a group of Asian children in their schoolyard . . . taken an assault rifle to . . . like bringing candy? What was happening to the language? It didn't mean what it said anymore; it meant the latest violence.

Those sisters who watched television brought it up at recreation. Was it happenstance that they were Asian children? They would never know; the man shot himself. Whoever cut off the hands and feet, did he leave them at the turn instead of killing himself? Was he seeking attention? Was he an errand boy for whoever severed them? Did he hate those people? Did the man with the AK-47 Russian-make assault rifle hate those children? She shook her head to clear her brain. The vestment she was working for the Bishop's Christmas Mass . . . she must finish that today.

By noon on Tuesday, all the roads in Westchester were lined with cars. People had crawled, in some instances on all fours, to bus and train stations, leaving their locomotion wherever it slithered and stopped. Freeze-thaw-freeze was becoming the byword for weather.

Mir agreed to stay on in Manhattan and clear an unexpected proofreading obstacle from Lawrence's desk. He was back from his sick bed but still not in great form. Since she had no one working late to read to, she would have to be extra careful not to make mistakes.

Senior Detective Eliaphus Daniel Janah wrestled the chains onto the Nissan Sentra and headed out to St. Hilary's.

Halfway to St. Hilary's, Eli passed Rapunzel's. No one was shopping today and there were spaces everywhere. He quickly pulled parallel to the curb and walked back to the twin towers. A very heavy coil of rope, braided and varnished, ran from the second floor of the building down one of the towers to the sidewalk. A simple brass plaque reading 'Rapunzel's' was fastened to the other tower.

Very elite. Only once in his lifetime had he been inside the door, and that had been a time when he did not have a cent to his name, beleaguered with bills that five children make who wear eyeglasses, grow crooked teeth, and break arms doing Lord knows what. But because of something he saw in Mir's eyes . . . he had taken a small loan out and come in here to purchase a gift certificate. He had remembered the way her eyes swung to the front door whenever they drove by. On the Feast of Lights, he left the gift certificate on top of the clothes hamper.

She was aglow that night. He smiled, remembering the woman who always said she didn't care about clothes dancing about their bedroom modeling her purchases. He should have done it more often.

The young woman facing him had a tremendous amount of eye makeup on. Lazily her lashes rose, weighted Egyptian fans, and slowly . . . coyly . . . they fell. Of course she would assist him; she would keep in mind that the lady he spoke of was slightly shorter.

He chose two lovely white tops, one a flowing silk and the other a very soft linen with little white rosebuds embroidered about the square neck. A deep purple cotton skirt with a tribal motif was the closest he could find to the one Marion had worn; they had nothing in paisley. Then he saw a soft faun brushed denim and bought that too. He wrote, 'In case blueberries do not wash out, E. J. on a card which he enclosed in an envelope, asked the sales woman to gift wrap and deliver to the address he wrote on her pad. He paid for it and was gone, leaving the young woman looking wistfully at his back.

Mrs. Berens opened the door of the rectory. "Afternoon, why don't you come in, Detective, place is quiet right now, boys all off. We could use the TV room." Boys? She wasn't exactly smiling, but she did seem more amenable than she had the other day. Letting her call the shots on time and place appeared to have paid off.

125

"Can I make you some tea?"

"That would be nice; it's quite miserable out there."

She nodded, directing him to the soft chair in the room with the fireplace, and continued on out back to the kitchen. She must have had the kettle on, for she returned almost immediately carrying a small tray, which held a tea pot, cups and saucers, and a small plate of cookies.

As he helped her place the kettle and the dish of butter cookies on the table in front of the sofa, Eli felt her eyes on him. He chose the easy chair and immediately sank almost completely to the floor. Mrs. Berens chose a straight chair, pulled it around to face him, and sat above him there, like the avenging angel or the ticket collector at the door. So much the better.

"Mrs. Berens, how long have you worked here at the rectory?" Her face, already pinched and wary, drew in at the edges. He saw a furtive animal for a moment, opossum or ferret; it embarrassed him. This reaction always embarrassed him. It was not altogether fear of law enforcement, he knew that from long experience. More, innate dis-ease. Something people couldn't cope with showing.

He wanted to look away, pretend he'd not seen the canker. Instead, he settled more comfortably back on the floor, stretched his long legs out, and sipped the tea. "Ahh, that's good."

The drawn lines about her eyes and jaw relaxed a little. "Seventeen years."

"Do you like it?"

"It's OK. Widow women can't complain."

He decided to wade right in, "What do you think of the delivery at the Annunciation?"

She seemed to have been expecting more questions about herself. She shifted on the chair and pulled her skirt down further over her knees. "What's there to think?" He waited. She hadn't taken any of her tea. The cup rattled against the saucer as she picked it up and drank it. He listened to her swallow. "They been courting it. A long time now they been asking for something jus' like this."

"Who, Mrs. Berens?"

She seemed to think about it for a long moment, "Those that don't belong, Detective. Foreigners taking our men's jobs, taking our houses we can't afford to live in no more, buying up our land for their Buddha monasteries. Where they getting the money? Third world they call 'em . . . hah!"

"I understand the sisters at the monastery have helped some people from Southeast Asia re-locate here."

"Humph! House of prayer they call themselves, that's a laugh. Their fault really, should have left well enough alone. When I first came here, I kept quiet. The old monsignor let it be known he didn't much care what my personal opinion was long as I kept it to myself."

She nibbled on the inside of her mouth. "But I seen too much since then. Should never have brought those children over. If those women had only stayed where they belonged *inside* the cloister, praying like they should, never would have happened." She seemed lost in thought. "Poor boys coming here don't know, young boys . . . trying to be a priest today . . . lots of confusion." She shook her head, then looked at him, a peaked smile playing about her narrow lips. "My Billy was going to be a priest, you know. Couldn't keep him when the war broke out."

"Which war?"

"Vietnam. He was killed over there." She licked her lower lip. "These boys . . . so much like Billy."

Eli, watching her, began to see where she could conceivably have been someone's mother . . . at one time . . . a long time ago. "Mrs. Berens, were you here at the rectory on the afternoon in question?"

"No, I already told you I visit my sister Tuesdays."

"When did you leave for your sister's?

And by the way, may I have her name and address."

"The plumber came that day, I wanted to watch him. Pokey, he worked like he was being paid time and a half. I left after he was finished, after I made sure he did the job . . . about one o'clock."

"Who was here when you left?

Mrs. Berens thought for a moment. "Father Strisbel was out making sick calls. Father Allen was heading over to the elementary to coach basketball. Touranment's next week. Father Elias had the books to balance."

He would check her sister's.

He would check that the basketball team had indeed received the benefits of Father Allen's coaching that afternoon.

And he could see that unless Father Elias came up with someone, no one was going to be able to vouch for his whereabouts that afternoon.

"Mrs. Berens, I'm sorry about your son." She had reverted. The frosty look she gave him said she cared less than a split pea what he was sorry about. "Thank you for giving me time on your day off. I may call you again as the investigation progresses." He played a game with his thighs, daring them to raise him from the hole he was in. They tightened, took the bit and ran with it. Mrs. Berens' eyes widened as he came up before her all in one movement.

It was almost midnight when Mir finished proofreading The *Empirical Epistemology of Epicurean Womanhood* by Evra Wimin. The article had given her a giant headache. It went on and on and on. Gad, what she was learning about bad writing. If she was home now she would walk out over the fields, climb a few fences, go to the State Forest. Walk, walk, walk. She couldn't see herself going back to the tiny room at Pius. Putting on her coat and hat, locking up the office, she started walking South, down lower Park instead of westward toward the Hudson.

She was walking fast onto Fourth when she realized she'd never seen CBGD's, only heard her sons refer to it. That's what she needed: loud, loud music, Suczzy or no. In a moderate rainfall, amid whispering car treads, she pulled the brim of the floppy wool hat down to shield her face, dug her hands deep in her pockets, and pretended she was heading to Battery Park, all stops loosed.

Her long legs gobbled up the blocks. An innate sense told her when to cross. Black piles of snow were shoved every which way to enable the traffic to pass, but not the people. Sewers were blocking up, water ankle-deep rising at the crossings. She laughed at the appalling mess of it all.

At Cooper Square, a black man came up to her and said something about food. She pulled her hands out of her pockets and waved them emptily in the air. She wasn't prepared; her wallet stuffed too deep in her rear pants pocket to pull it out there in the street.

At Jones St. three young men pushed her, forcing her to climb a snow bank. She caught her balance and counted off the streets to Bleecker, in her head. CBGB's should be on the next block.

Mirari Buttrick Janah always told herself that she kept out

of trouble by gauging the prevalent vibes. As she approached Bleecker, she put all her antennae out. If the place was really as scuzzy as all that, she would walk quickly past it westward and on to Pius.

She was talking thus to herself when she saw Arthur Danley. He was striding from Second Avenue, crossing Bowery, about to enter Bleecker. Excitedly, she started to hail him when a man grabbed his arm. Danley knew him, something was said, a right arm to right arm clasp was exchanged. They headed together along Bleecker, westward.

Quickly, she walked to the corner and peered down the block. Danley stood to the side of the lighted entranceway to CBGB's talking to three men. As one looked down the block toward her, she instinctively faded back against the service door to her right.

For about five minutes, they stood in the muted light off to the side of the main entrance, while the rain fell. Danley and the man who had clasped his arm at the intersection were both about six foot one, well built. The other two were slightly shorter. These last wore camouflage pants and laced paratrooper boots. When they moved their feet, the light from the door of CBGB's glistened on the wet leather. The man who had met Danley back at the corner turned to the side. His hair was slicked back, long and wet, and the nose was the most outstanding Roman nose she had seen outside of the blurb on the jacket of the Collected Works of Marcus Aurelius.

She was suddenly aware of a man close to her face eyeing her. He started to pull his wallet from his pants pocket, fumbling under a dirty raincoat. Shaking her head quickly from left to right, she put a large sick smile on her face. He quickly moved on.

When she looked westward again toward hardcore hall, there were only two bikers standing, slapping each other on the shoulder in the light from the doors.

Her eyes hadn't been off the four men for more than a minute and a half. No longer visible on the street, they must have gone inside. It didn't feel right; she discarded the initial impulse to follow them. Danley hadn't exactly lied, but it was fairly clear he had no intention of bringing her here. A hangout? Distorted percussion reached her, followed by a wail that could have been a human on drugs or a guitar. No longer interested in loud music, she wondered about the men he had met. For a bishop, he got around.

Pulling the hat down over her forehead, she walked quickly in the direction of the two leather-jacketed bikers. A low whistle as she approached made her glance up in time to swerve neatly out from the arm wearing the leather-spike bracelet flung in her path. She did not break stride, but kept moving fast down Bleecker toward Lafayette to Washington Square beyond. Very seldom is a target moving that fast followed.

"Deo gratias."

"Reverend Mother, my name is Mirari Buttrick. As I told the sister, I'm a freelance writer. No, I understand. I don't mind waiting until you clear it with His Reverence. I spoke to him a couple of days ago. The phone company will be connecting my home phone this afternoon. No, I'm not new to the area. I've spent most of my life here. I've been working and living in the City for the past three years. You might say I've decided to move out to give my soul a rest." No harm in a few brownie points. "My number will be 761-8888."

Thanking her, she hung up the pay phone. Having deposited two dollars in quarters just to hold . . . when she could have run the eight miles up the road . . . she was not impressed at the speed at which the sisters moved. Fortunately, the operator did not ring back for more money.

It was good, though, to grab the early train out of the City. Lawrence was pleased that she finished the job. More likely he's seen the time and a half I've put in . . . decided he would even cut the pay by giving me the afternoon off, she thought. Tch, tch my dear, are we getting a bit sour? No way! Pragmatic is all. She would do a little food shopping and grab a taxi up the hill.

The taxi driver took one look at the driveway and whistled, "Lady, I'd rather not tackle *that!*"

"S'OK." She paid him, he drove off, and all was still.

The drive curving up to the house looked narrow. Freezing rain and sleet had brought the trees together. From either side, they leaned on each other, rigorously interlacing. Those that found no support cascaded into the opening that was the driveway. This fabric of frozen, clinking daggers swayed, playing wind-chime magic.

Snow was deep, unbroken, but for tracks up and down one side. She crunched along, parting the waterfall with her gloved hand.

Clam and Chowder's heads swung langorously . . . a regal boredom in their eyes—'Oh well . . . she's home'—as only cats can humph. They stood and stretched. One at a time they jumped, rubbed against her legs, flag up, followed her to the bathroom where they sat patiently, one on either side, listening to her tinkle. The little ritual performed, intimacy reestablished, they shadowed her for the rest of the afternoon until she fed them.

132

Chapter Twelve

"John, how many unofficial contacts have we in Southeast Asia? Rather not go the usual routes, no police computers, OK? Talk more later."

Eli had made four phone calls so far that morning. Woke at five, stripped, exercised on the mat in the cold, dark room. When he had worked up a sufficient sweat, he lit a small candle and let the Tai Chi weave him a body. Form, tempo, shape, the space directions . . . wind-song dynamic finding balance by continuously flowing.

While the kettle boiled, he went into the bedroom to the bookshelves for the I Ching. Bypassing a tall cylindrical crock full of varying lengths of yarrow stalks, their prickly ends skyward, he glanced at the one stalk lying on the floor, the one always put aside from the forty-nine. He reached for the coins. Easier to throw them in the breakfast nook, on the table.

Tao is obscured. You fix your eyes on little segments of existence only.

True quiet means keeping still. When the time has come to keep still.

Going forward. When the time has come to go forward.

You will then be in agreement with the demands of the time.

Your attention should center not on things in their state of being. It should center on their movement in change.

This last set caused such a prickling along his scalp that he laughed out loud.

What did it mean?

He didn't know yet. Pouring himself another cup of coffee, he reached reflectively for the red lacquer piece hanging on the side wall. Standing woman, in life force color of blood, gazed contemplatively off into the distance. She gave only her shadow side, repelling yang influences. He held her with long slender fingers for some minutes, then decisively turned the talisman. Jade lady looked directly at him across the breakfast table.

They had directed him to a side door for deliveries and repairmen. 'Peace' it said, in black letters. He wondered if that calmed the carpenter, the plumber, the furnace man encountering the faceless, black-veiled moving figures ringing the warning bells. A man afoot within the cloister.

When the door opened, the young workman, looking dubious, followed his older, casual, evidently more seasoned compatriot across the threshold into the cloister. He glanced back at Eli. His plumber's basket hit the door jamb. His eyes went skyward.

When Sister Damian of Mary opened the tiny, shuttered window to the side of the door, she looked as if she'd been running. At least she looked warm.

Eli was cold.

"Detective Janah, I'm sorry to have to bring you back here. There's no heat in this wing." She didn't have to tell him that. "We never got around to insulating that outside wall.

"We have a visiting scriptural scholar with us," she said proudly. "He's using the speak this morning. A sister's brother. How are you? How are things going?' She didn't wait for him to answer. "The investigation has been pressing on my mind."

Eli was quiet. Sister Damian launched into a fast-paced monologue salted with little fact and peppered heavily with female intuition. The intuitive, the female, looked at him with troubled grey eyes. Looked directly, as the Jade Lady had earlier that morning.

"I am refusing to see something, Detective, I just *know* it. This usually means I don't want to see it." She was extremely antsy. "You know, Detective Janah, the sisters don't usually go overseas. Although we've been embroiled in that part of the world now for some years, we haven't needed to go because we've been blessed with some very fine clergy totally involved in our work. Almost all the arrangements and most of the traveling necessary to bring these good people out from under some horrendous situations, has been done by them.

"I've been in Pusan, that's South Korea, and Bangkok. A couple of the sisters had to go to Chau Doc in Cambodia. They made it out safely just an hour before the Khmer forces brought an offensive against the harbor. An hour," she repeated it softly. "They and the children would have perished." She looked at him through the tiny window with the makeshift grill to see if he appreciated the providence of this. Then, as if seeing something for the first time on his face, she looked hurriedly away down to some point on the floor on her side of the wall.

"Sister, is there anything I should know?"

Worriedly, she looked up again. "I'm sure he knew me." She hesitated, "He was sorry he had to leave his grisly package on our doorstep so to speak. It was a warning that it's over."

"What's over?"

Sister Damian could not say it. She looked him straight in the eye and said, "I don't know." He saw the set jaw.

"Who made the delivery?"

"I don't know."

She didn't know *why*, he thought. Until she knows why she is not going to say. "Sister, sometimes the most seemingly in-consequential things help in an investigation like this."

"Yes, I'm aware of that, Detective. The light dawns slowly though," she shrugged. "That's the way I am. I'll be sure to call you if the wattage goes up." It was more of a grimace than a smile.

Laconically, Eli said to himself, She'll call when she's got it solved. Why must everyone play secret sleuth???

Back in the open by the car, he smiled. He had found out what he needed. When he called asking to see her for a few moments, he meant exactly that. If she hadn't opened her mouth, he would have been content. It was all over her face. He could read.

She was beginning to see something too big to swallow. Yes. People think evil opens doors but it seldom does, it doesn't need to, there are too many 'good' out there doing the acting.

March winds . . . Standing fronting them upon the grit of sand and salt, he held unsteady footing. He watched the wind buckle around the brick of the old, brown monastery buildings. The chapel door opened. There was a gust of song, and Father Elias stepped out.

A look of displeasure flitted across his face. He erased it. "Looking for me, Detective?"

Go with it, Eli . . . "As a matter of fact, yes Father, I was. But I heard about the visiting scriptural scholar and wasn't sure you'd be here."

Elias didn't comment but searched Eli's face. "What did you want to see me about?"

Eli's hand closed around the car keys. "When did your brother die, Father? What year? And where exactly?

Emotions chased each other across the priest's features. "He died in 1965. His Phantom 4 crashed on a run south of Da Nang among the mountains along the coast."

"You said he died slowly?" Elias looked at him questioningly.

"I did? Probably meant we died slowly, waiting. No, he was killed instantly. You see, we received conflicting news. He crashed. He died. He lived and walked away. It wasn't until 1967 that we heard—this time they were sure, they said—that he'd been killed in the crash." He gave a bitter half laugh." Life teaches you not to believe all you hear."

You're not going to make it easy for me are you, Eli thought, but instead he said, "I'll go with that. Where were you, Father, the Tuesday afternoon the hands and feet were delivered to the turn room?"

"At my desk in the rectory doing up the books, trying to stretch the money ten ways." The answer came back very fast, it was almost curt.

"Can anyone vouch for that?"

"If you mean did anyone watch me while I sat there, no.

Mrs. Berens left to visit her sister around one, and it was quiet in the rectory until Bill returned from sick calls around four. No one dropped by. There were no phone calls."

"You caught up on the books?"

"Yes."

Mirari was hunched reflectively in front of the Valery article. In the distance she could hear the fire crackling in the living room. This room was cold. It was off limits to Clam and Chowder. The article, spread out on the long table under the spotlights, was cold and white. Was it real? The mark of the real is total insignificance. She shook her head and lectured Paul Valery mentally for that enigmatic saying, 1944 . . . Old man, you were becoming a mystic.

Her preoccupation was interrupted by a curious buzzing. It sounded like the copy machine had run out of paper . . . but she didn't have a copy machine! Phone! She now had a phone. But who on earth knew?

"Ms. Buttrick? This is Reverend Mother Michaels. I hope this isn't a bad time to call. I always seem to have more time after Compline to make my calls."

The soft voice continued, "Ms. Buttrick, I must tell you I was not at all enthralled to have someone writing about us." There was a long hesitant silence. "But . . . after speaking with His Reverence Bishop Danley, I am somewhat reassured. He is probably right when he says it is only a matter of time, and that there will be others. He feels confident of the quality of your work. He tells me sensationalism is just not your line, that there is an intelligence and thoughtfulness . . . moreover a sensitivity . . . that I shall be relieved to find." Mir heard the nun take a deep breath.

"He also assures me that you will be the one writer allowed to handle the matter, that we can justifiably turn any others away. This you can be sure is a relief to me. Is there anything you want to ask me at this time?"

Mir, who had been silent, was cursing Danley. Gad, what a build-up, who did he think she was, Saint Teresa? How could anyone write what they had to and still keep within the perameters he had just set down? Stick him! she thought. She realized the nun was waiting, so she hauled her temper off the ceiling and in a very modulated soft voice, said, "No, Reverend Mother, I can't think of anything at this time. Now that you've given me the go-ahead, I'm very grateful by the way, I'll start work on the outline and begin researching the history of the Congregation, the background material you understand."

"I'm putting one of our sisters at your disposal, Ms. Buttrick. She can get you the archives. We keep them here at the Annunciation. Her name is Sister Damian of Mary. I have told her you will be calling."

When Mir hung up the phone, she sat watching the play of the flames in the fireplace. So. She had her next assignment. It came to her from the faceless sisters, the fates, without the usual freelancer's hustle. Way to go! Which one of her sons used that all the time?

The phone startled her. "Arthur Danley, Mirari," the jovial voice boomed. "Thought I'd catch you at Pius, but they said you'd checked out already. I want you to come to this opening tomorrow night. So, what?" His manner was cheerfully indifferent. "So you went back up to Westchester, so, you come back down." His manner softened. "Come on Mir, I've gotta go out of town Friday, be gone for at least a week. The artist's name is Zhang Wei. You'll like him. Visually abstract, he's Western and yet, his brushwork is very Zen." His voice became teasing. "Lots of that nothingness you talk about. Come on. I'll take you out to dinner. You're not getting fat. OK, I'll take you to El Faro, Spanish, not Italian. Great place, been there in the Village sixty years."

"You haven't let me say anything."

"What's to say?"

"How did you get my number? It's not cold yet; the guy just hooked it up."

"Ahh . . . connections."

"Arthur, I can't afford to come in as much any more . . ."

"I'll put you up." She didn't answer. "No strings."

"I can't stay at the bishop's mansion."

"Who said anything about the manse. I'll put you up at my place, got an extra room." "I'd like to have you there . . . yes, I'd like that very much. I'll meet the train. If I'm late, hit the information."

As Eli came even with the lieutenant's door, he caught the rapid arm wave that meant he was being summoned. "Janah . . . humn, the lieutenant coughed. "Humn . . . did you know the captain's Catholic?" The lieutenant frowned.

Eli leaned forward, nonplussed, "Catholic?"

The lieutenant wagged his head, "Catholic."

They were silent. The lieutenant doodled on his pad as Eli watched the pursed lips and wondered how long the head was going to go on emphasizing, nod, nod, nod.

"I don't know if I knew that." The wagging said he should know it. He waited

"Eli, (first names now) the captian read your report on the

Annunciation business." A long pause followed. The lieutenant took a deep breath. "He seems to feel you're spending an unnecessarily large amount of time looking into the lives of the clergy." Warily, he looked at Eli. "You feel this is so?"

"No."

"You don't huh, humn." The lieutenant paused. "There is quite a bit there, Eli." He said, gesturing to the report lying open on his blotter, "on our Archdiocesan finest." Eli's face remained infuriatingly calm. Abruptly, the lieutenant sat up straight and said authoritively, "You have a theory then that calls for investigation along these lines?"

"Yes."

"Eli, listen, if the captain's beloved clergy are implicated, it better be good, it better be damn good; otherwise there'll be hell to pay."

Eli gave him a level look. "I'll keep that in mind."

"You do that. That's all."

Walt Bath and John Fay had watched the little scene. When he reached their nest of desks, their eyes were on him questioningly.

"Captain feels we should stick to investigating the laity."

"Oh?" It was unanimous. "Well . . . I bet they don't move around as much." Bath was fiddling with a small mountain of papers. "Visas . . . travel permits . . . passports, the morning was a revelation. Good thing some guys owe me."

"I kinda think we're doing very well, myself . . ." Eli said, staring inscrutably at the In box. "In fact, I feel better and better. We may have to keep some of our findings under our hats . . . we'll see . . ." Fay and Bath looked at each other.

"What have we got so far?" Fay spoke. "We have half a dozen firm contacts, guys with good eyes and good ears who want to remain unidentified. One each in Thailand, Laos, South Korea, North Vietnam . . . two in Cambodia."

"We need some homegrown information," said Eli. "What did people over there think about this re-location business the Congregation of Prompt Succor has been engaged in. We need to find those who are missing hands and feet."

"We're dealing with a very well traveled group," Bath said. "Father Elias went overseas for the first time in '67. Laos. He accompanied a guy by name of Maysenrod, Bob Maysenrod. I'll check him out. He didn't go again until '74, when he went with Monsignor O'Reilly. After that, O'Reilly went every year and he went with him."

Bath checked his notes, "He went alone in '82. And again in '85, '86, '87. Late October '87."

"I'd like to know exactly what he did on those trips," Eli said.

Bath raised an eyebrow.

O'Reilly was very well traveled! Makes you wonder how he got a parish. Between 1950 and 1981 he was in some part of Korea, Indochina, or Asia at least once a year.

"Father Strisbel, on the other hand, made two trips to Cambodia fifteen years ago, came home, started his blood-pouring, and hasn't been overseas since.

"Jeff Allen has been to Ireland and Turkey, not Asia.

"Father Polaski has been to China, Cambodia, and Laos . . . one, two, three. Once to China, twice to Cambodia, three times to Laos. Two years ago he went to Nicaragua. Last year he returned."

Eli, juggling little clerical hats around on his pad, looked like he was playing tic tac toe. He looked up, "How about Danley?"

Bath took a deep breath. "Danley . . . well . . . His Reverence tops the Monsignor. Ten years after he quit the Marines, he was back in Asia as some sort of liaison between Bishop's Relief and the Eastern churches. He's been there ever since. He's worn out more passports than a prom queen's slippers. His name is always mentioned with some good: he's flying foodstuffs in, ferrying medical supplies, bargaining with a rebel chieftain for the lives of a group of peasant peoples, relocating homeless." Bath hesitated, scowling at the toe of his shoe. "One of our contacts says that in three instances, tribal states folded, government kaput, immediately after Danley left the area with his orphans." He looked up then, eyebrows raised.

First thing Thursday morning, Mir called the Monastery of the Annunciation and asked for Sister Damian of Mary. They made an appointment for one p.m. At ten to one, Mir parked her car in front of the chapel and got out. She felt the silence. So this is where the other half went, she thought. Raising the kids those crazy years, was this what she had longed for?

Gazing at the huge bar and grill structure in the speak, Mir thought, how psychologically potent! Separation. Austerity. Here they were staring you in the face. No wonder the new graphic computers play so much with symbol. Efficient, neat, the concept in the gut.

Her thoughts were interrupted by footsteps on the other side and the sound of wooden panels banging together. A deep, soft voice spoke, "Ms. Buttrick, is that you?" She felt silly answering yes; who else would it be? The disembodied voice almost instantly became a beam of light, a hand, breaking through the blackness. It pulled the curtain aside. A hand rolling a curtain, looped black material through a piece of grillwork.

The hand belonged to the tallest nun she had ever seen. Mir was not used to being looked down upon by other women. There was a smile in the clear grey eyes as Sister Damian, introducing herself, looked down.

She did not open all the shutters, but left the panels to her right closed. In the smaller space, she looked bigger than life. She invited Mir to pull a chair up to the opened side of the grillwork.

Watching her sweep the scapular on the long, grey habit out from under her, sit down and fold the frontispiece on her knees, Mir thought, Regal. She moved like a queen.

"I thought we might talk for a while, Ms. Buttrick. You could tell me a little of what you have in mind." She sighed, "I'll put in my two cents worth, so to speak, and," she threw her long, slender fingers in the air, "we'll see what kind of stew we concoct." Sister Damian sat there grinning.

Mir had a feeling her eyes were wide. This nun hadn't been sitting twiddling her thumbs when she spoke to Reverend Mother last evening. Yet here she was, plucked from her work, sent to face a stranger at a ticklish time, cheerful as can be. So this is what obedience is.

"Before you leave, I'll dig the Constitution out of the basement. And there are half a dozen accounts of the early days of the order. For now, why don't I just shut my mouth and let you talk."

There was a strangeness in talking to someone through all this somber grillwork, but quicker than she would have thought, Mir forgot it was there.

At one point, Sister Damian referred to the investigation.

She mentioned Eli by name and instinctively, Mirari refrained from letting on she knew him. At three-thirty, when a bell caused her to glance at the clock, she was startled. There was barely time to make the four o'clock into New York. Saying a quick good-bye, 'Some other day for the archives!'—she was gone.

Chapter Thirteen

Eliaphus Daniel Janah was driving slowly and reflectively along the lower portion of Briar Creek Road when an old Buick careened out of a side street, cut him off, and spewed oily smoke in his face. Until the windshield cleared, he cursed the driver. When he realized it was Mirari, he suddenly wanted very much to see her.

She was bearing rapidly toward the house. Give her a few minutes, he thought, slowing the Nissan. The blue Buick disappeared.

He no sooner got within sight of the old driveway than she hurtled out of it, turned and went racing off in the direction of the train station South of town.

He stepped on the gas. Where was she going now? Hadn't Zeke told him she stayed in Westchester Thursdays? The woman was impossible. They hadn't spoken in six months. He had no idea if she was well. She never asked for money; was she making enough to make ends meet?

Eli wasn't sure afterwards why he parked the car in the rear lot, checked his billfold, grabbed a small overnight case from the trunk, and boarded the four o'clock to New York, keeping surreptitiously to the rear.

He thought of those early years in the city. Young, foolishly in love, they saved up for a sitter and got a room in the Village for the night. Suppose they just happened to run into each other again. A little blue flame of hopefulness burned in his chest; all things seemed possible.

He looked at his features in the glass against the becoming darkness. Older, not necessarily wiser. He missed her in his life.

As the train sped south, a wry smile played around the corners of his mouth. She was probably meeting some guy, some artsy type, a writer, painter. God knows; With Mir, a rock musician was possible. He could tell already, he'd be on the return train. At least he had a book in the tote. He gave a great sigh, chalking it up to experience!

Mir, collapsing in one of the front cars, let her mind go blank. The conductor spoke three times, then, unable to break through the glaze on the attractive face, he finally shook her shoulder. She pulled her mind away from the monastery.

The train, descending into the dingy alley that was Harlem, brought her to the present. Some heavy duty communication had taken place back there. Sister Damian had wanted to talk. The two and a half hours went like minutes; her mind was racing. Better let it go now. Relax. Enjoy Danley's exuberant maleness.

Once Eli convinced himself he was bumbling into a tryst, he kept well behind her in the crowd leaving the train at Grand Central. She was walking spiritedly toward the main information desk when he saw her arm go up in greeting. Arthur Danley bore down on her. Eli stopped abruptly.

A woman's voice behind him said, "Hey mister, watch it!" He stood watching the look on Danley's face. A bear of a guy;

he saw him put his hand on Mir's fly-away shoulder-length greying-red hair as if to tame it. Danley's head bent. At fifty feet, their laughter pierced Eli.

In Grand Central, Arthur Danley looked at her as if she were a newly discovered passage to ancient China.

"It does great things for my ego, Arthur D. to see you standing there grinning like that."

Making a curiously inept gesture at smoothing her hair, he bent down. "Very glad you decided to come! Here, let me take that, I've a car in the garage across the way."

He sat looking at her in the black Lincoln, "How do you feel about going straight to El Faro? Or do you want to freshen up somewhere first?"

"Let's go to El Faro. I can do whatever needs doing there. I've been running all day, just barely made the train."

"Seems to me that's the usual state of affairs with you, you're always running," but his eyes were frankly appraising.

""I said I was going to eat sparingly, but I'm starved. I want you to order me a dry, dry martini straight up, while I'm primping. I'm going to eat, I'm going to drink, I'm going to celebrate my new assignment!" She sat back against the soft, tan leather upholstery with a satisfied smile on her face. The back of his powerful hand caressed her cheek slowly, coming to rest on her lips.

She had watched his profile as he maneuvered the luxury car through rush hour traffic. He enjoyed every minute of it. A fine color inched along the broad cheekbones. Some of his actions had reminded her of Anthony Quinn, like how his eyes shone every time he stole an inch of someone's space, or cut someone off without the brush on brush of metal. She felt wellbeing seep through her limbs. She had long since stopped questioning it. A powerful man handling a powerful car was definitely a turn-on.

""Don't forget the martini, please?" He nodded. "I'll be back in a few minutes." She made her way from the table in the semi-private dining room to the ladies' room.

Well! Mir looked at herself, You look like you've run the thirty mile and won. The clothes one wears to an interview at a monastery are not the ones to wear to dinner with a man like Arthur Danley, my dear. She put her case down on the table, slid out of the high-necked sweater, sniffed her armpits, decided she smelled OK, and pulled a red, scoop-necked, silk velour from the overnight bag and drew it on.

It went well with the black skirt. After putting on tiny, pierced ruby earrings, she bent her head low and brushed the hell out of her hair. Straightening up, she ran fingers coated with gel through it.

He watched her walk up the three wide steps, watched her walk every single inch of flooring to the table, with a flare behind his eyes. When she sat down, he made a pretext of knocking ash from his cigar. Gruffly, he spoke to the table, "That was *not* judicious."

"Not discreet? Or not wise? Women celebrating is always innate Wisdom." A teasing smile played around her eyes as she faced the glare in his.

Arthur Danley looked slowly from the top of her head to the low-slung breasts to the twin pinpricks of red in her ear lobes and gave a long drawn-out sigh. He was drinking some kind of black ale.

Gently she tapped her martini glass on his, "Cheers."

The colorless liquid leapt over the rim, the droplets flashing in the candle light before soaking in the padded tablecloth as he grabbed her wrist and held it for a long moment. "Order for me?" she said. "Not too hot."

"I can see why," he said, laughing at her across the table. Her cheeks were flushed, her eyes sparkled. "That martini has gone straight to your head hasn't it?"

She nodded in mock submission. They ate in silence for some time.

"You do know your way around the better restaurants, Arthur D."

"I know my way around the poorer ones also."

"I believe it," she mumbled through a mouthful. She did not mention seeing him on Bleecker.

"So, you had your first meeting with the sisters at Annunciation Monastery today. How did it go?" He stretched back, opened his suit jacket and stuck his thumbs in his belt.

"Pretty well, I'm excited, could have killed you though, with that build-up!" She frowned at him. "I walked in there so overwhelmingly conscious of my lack of sensationalism, my thoughtfulness, and my sensitivity, that I nearly tripped over my feet." He leaned across the table suddenly and slowly ran a finger softly down one side and up the other of the cleft of her breasts. "Oh no, don't do that. You have to be wearing the right uniform for that." She laughed to herself and then shook her head as if trying to scatter some thought from her brain.

"What are you thinking?" he said.

"Noooo."

"Come on."

The martini, the wine, the food, the man, the air of seduction, lessened her inhibitions. "I had this fantasy." The waiter came and removed their plates. They ordered espresso. His large, powerful hands were clasped an inch from her breasts on the cleared white tablecloth; curly gold hairs sparkled on their backs.

"Yes?"

"I saw myself kneeling, kissing your ring. You were piously fondling my breasts."

Flares leapt like incendiary bombs in his eyes. "When did you start having these thoughts, my child?"

She choked, "That's it! That's it exactly, that's the Voice! They would sit there behind the velvet curtains in their little cubicles asking all sorts of impertinent questions. How long did I think of it. What did I do when I thought of it. Did I stop doing it before I finished thinking . . . Oh, God! Impurity. I know what impurity is. One day, an old priest, after long nit-picky questioning, started breathing heavily. Suddenly, he was wheezing." She gave an imitation at the table. "I up and left."

"What were you telling the poor fellow?"

"Nothing worth wheezing about."

"Maybe it was your perfume."

"No. He asked one hell of a lot of questions." He was looking at her fondly. "Oh, Arthur, I'm sorry! I've had too much to drink. It's your bag, I mean, I'm an idiot to knock your livelihood. I've known some amazingly beautiful men in the priesthood . . ."

"Don't!" Two fingers came down on her lips. "I've been many things, Mir. I grew up in alleys. I've worn rags, I've worn rings. It's all a game. I'm not attached . . . Ahh, since we're being honest tonight, hell, I'm damn attached . . . I'm attached to the power that comes with it, the freedom it allows."

He changed the subject. "You think you're going to enjoy doing the article?" She nodded. "Did you know your ex was in charge of the investigation?

"Yes, I guess I did hear that."

"What's he like?"

"Eli? Oh . . ." Arthur Danley watched her closely. "Eli's a curious amalgam." She grew serious. "He's very good at what he does."

"But lousy at being a husband?"

She ran her tongue along her lower lip. "Sometimes I think he married me in order to study Kaballah. Did you know you cannot study Kaballah unless you're married?"

Danley was cautious . . . "Is it a turn-on?"

He got what he wanted when she laughed out loud. "Yes! I'm not being fair, Arthur, not fair at all. We loved each other. He married me, took on two kids, made a home for the rest that came along. My first husband just up and left one day, I was just a kid myself. Her voice softened. "Eli's Eli . . ."

"Do you see him?"

"Not much at all. It's been at least six months since we talked." "Seems to me . . . seeing the care in your eyes . . . you should keep in touch." He did not look at her as he said this.

She whispered in return, "Is that pastoral advice, Your Reverence?"

He didn't smile, but looked steadily at her. "What I'd like to do right now could not, under existing sanctions, be called pastoral. Would you like brandy with your coffee?"

"Please."

Some men don't know the first thing about seduction, Mir thought, watching his hands on the brandy bottle the waiter had left at a sign from him, on the table. And then, there are men like this. A curly fleece escaped from the cuffs of his shirt.

"I am grateful for the introduction to Mother Michaels," Mir said. "She'd have had nothing to do with me without your say. It will put food on the table."

"You'll do good work and rather you than some harebrain."

"How did you decide to become a priest?"

He tried to be jocular. "Have we had that much to drink?"

"You needn't answer."

He looked at her seriously, "I've always been a wheeler and dealer. One day I decided to wheel and deal God. I'm good at it. One has to do what he can do well." He shrugged his shoulders. "In many ways, I'm still maneuvering as I did on the streets as a kid."

He changed the subject. "Still want to see my friend Zhang's work? His show's at the Caroline on Spring.

"Yes, I would like that." She was feeling very trusting and laid back. She wanted to stand by his side and feel the otherness of him. They could discuss the paradoxicality of Zen and Western abstract art. She wanted the slow burn to spread while they discussed the Eastern inspiration.

At the C. Hill Gallery, he moved her about through the crowd discussing expressionism and atypicality and synthesis and mountains and clouds and spirit and air. And every word said what his fingers were saying on her arm, her waist, her back. Every word said, I want you.

The on again off again drizzle had succeeded in saturating the shoulders of Eli's overcoat. A trickle of cold water gleefully found an opening at the seam between the collar and the body of the coat and poured onto not-so-warm flesh.

He felt cold, wet, angry, and disbelieving. If it had been anyone but Danley! He'd be home in his nice warm apartment with his feet up. The pipe dream about Mir, long burst, he settled into surveillance. He hadn't lost his touch, even the unroutine patrol hadn't spotted him.

While they ate and he held up a wall, an old friend at the Village precinct traced the car. The big, black Lincoln was registered to Maysenrod, Robert D.

Danley, his arm about Mir, was coming out of the gallery with three others. The five of them stood talking in the light rain. Then Mir and Danley walked towards the Lincoln. He slipped hurriedly down the side street, hailed a taxi, and was able to point the headlights of the big car out to his driver before it turned the corner and headed north.

Trailing Mirari like this left a bad taste in his mouth. She couldn't know what she'd gotten into!

He had a pretty good idea where they were heading. The address on the registration was one of those reclamation brownstone streets worth billions. He had the driver stop well out of sight, paid him, and began walking down the opposite side of the street. I wish I had a dog and a stack of newspapers, he thought. The brownstone, more elaborate than some of its neighbors, had a refurbished carriage house attached. He watched as it swallowed up the Lincoln.

As the doors folded down hiding the tail lights, he eyeballed his surroundings looking for a vantage point. There wasn't any. Then he saw the alley two houses up. It jutted toward the rear of the buildings.

Someone making a cursory attempt to separate garbage and keep it from the rain and the neighborhood cats and dogs had built a three-sided lean-to along Danley's garden fence. From there, he watched the windows on the second floor light up, watched the broad-shouldered proprietary way Danley pulled the drapes across the large center window as Mir walked up behind him.

Eli hunkered down with his back against the lean-to and asked himself what a sane man would do in a similar situation. He let all the muscles in his neck relax and willed the loosening ripple down his torso to that tip of spine nearest the dirt. A light spit . .

. spit . . . of water hit the lid of the can to his right. The hiss of tire noise on the wet streets sifted back to the little oasis.

If he hadn't been as still, inside and out, Eli would never have sensed the man. He didn't breathe and he made not one iota of sound. It was the void approaching soundlessly on his left that warned him. Letting the breath ease out of his lungs, he waited.

This wasn't just any man. No one moves *so* emptily without training. Lots of it. Most people did not realize how far their psychic body sticks out, a bundle of tentacles, pleasant or unpleasant, riffling the environment. Like Sister Damian's electromagnetic energy.

He smiled to himself, crouching there in the dark. Someone who could pull in so expertly, ahh . . . when had he last encountered one such as that? It had been a long time. Too long!

The surge brought him to his feet with one knee bent. Bursting skyward, the knee came up under the chin, even as his curved right hand crushed a nose. The figure slumped for just a moment, dazed, before he could make a comeback, Eli brought pressure on his neck until he crumpled. Catching him, he lowered him quietly to the ground.

It was over too quickly. He pulled the limp body into a bit

of light from the ground floor of the house across the way. A man measuring about six feet, dressed entirely in black, face black-stained, lay at his feet, his nose evidently broken.

No windows opened in the other apartments. The drizzle quickened and turned to drops. No use leaving him out in the wet. Eli pulled the limp body into the makeshift shelter.

He looked for long moments at the second-floor window. Could Mir take care of herself? He hoped so. A sixth sense told him to get out of there. He wondered if the man had seen him well enough to identify him. That would depend on how long he had been observed. He'd have to chance it; he certainly wasn't going to kill anyone tonight.

He made his desultory way out to the main avenue. He wasn't exactly a father waiting up for a daughter to return from a first date. Why did he feel like one? Aimlessly, he watched the traffic, then hailed a cab to take him to Grand Central Station.

As the train left the city, he got the book out. So the bishop's unofficial quarters came with a guard. And not just any guard. Someone trained by Special forces, trained in martial arts. How much was at stake guarding a bishop? He wondered if Walt Bath had anything on Maysenrod yet. The book lay unopened on his knees.

Chapter Fourteen

The old-fashioned cage elevator that took them from the garage to Danley's apartment had brass railings, and a gold snake with a mouth like a yawning cat glazing over in the center of the marble floor. Mir moved her feet.

"Something else, isn't he?"

"I don't think he wants me to stand on his head."

"Oh . . . I dunno, I'm sure he's gotten used to it after all these eons."

He opened the cage onto a hall with the softest, deepest, reddest carpet she had ever seen. Instinctively, she kicked off her shoes as her black coat slid off her shoulders. He watched the flush rise in her cheeks as she dug her stockinged toes into the pile.

"Well!" she exclaimed. And then, "I don't see a crucifix."

Arthur Danley was very quiet. He looked at the tall woman wearing the blouse the color of his rug for a long time before he reached out and drew her up against his hip. "Do you know you walk like a wild woman? You walk like an animal walks in deep wood. The first time I saw you, I saw a lioness." He chuckled, remembering, "trying to find something to eat in a very strange place. Did you ever eat the English muffin? Mine was dry."

Astride his thigh, she nibbled on his ear, "Like this?" She

listened to him moan. "I want to love you," she whispered. "Come see the apartment first. You have absolutely no restraint, you know."

"True, Your Reverence, true . . . Which is your room?"

The place was lovely, as old, well-kept buildings that have lots of money poured into them can be. High ceilings, tall windows, wainscotting, floor-to-ceiling bookshelves, wideboard plank flooring. The warm touch of wood from days when it was plentiful.

"It's beautiful!" she murmured. But he was looking at her. Feeling his eyes on her, she turned. "Which is your room?"

Unspeaking, he took her to the first room off the kitchen. "The bath attached to this connects with mine. I can lock the door between, let you have it. There's another bath," he finished lamely.

Placing her overnight case on the flat, wide surface of the bureau, coat and shoes in the closet, she turned to him waiting in the open doorway, and repeated: "Where's your room?"

The mixture of cigar smoke, leather, cologne, and maleness was as heavy as the fresh-ground coffee smell that hit you when you opened the door of the Cheese Emporium. The room was very large. He walked past the big centrally placed bed with its white comforter and pulled the drapes. Then he flicked the light on a shiny, dark wood stand. It held a blond wood box of Hava Yorcas.

A series of doors took up one wall. A brushwork diorama started working its myth out by the windows, continued the full length of the wall at the head of the bed, and ended at the doors. It appeared to be the story of a metamorphosis. A woodland scene . . . a waterfall . . . a hermit sitting in a house hidden partly by cloud, followed by a journey of what looked like Samurai warriors.

"It's beautiful!" she repeated. Pensively, she turned around surveying the room. "Do you keep clerical black here?"

Without opening his mouth, he took her by the hand to the farthest door. Half a dozen black suits hung beside twice as many rabats, four long black cassocks at the far end. She picked up the arm of one of the cassocks and felt the cloth.

"Please put on the black for me? Not the cassock, the suit . . . replete with collar." She felt the heat rising in her face. "I'll make coffee. Cognac?"

"Over the microwave," he said.

Mir, sitting in the large central room in the wing chair, her bare feet on the Persian rug, looked up when he came to the door. He was just as imposing and as much of an impostor as he had been that first day at Pius.

Rising from the chair, her glass in her left hand, she came forward holding out his tumbler of cognac. Standing tall before him, she almost reached his mouth. She didn't kiss him but put her finger in the liquid and spread it over his lower lip.

"You look extremely distinguished, you know." His eyes told her that he found that amusing, but also that she was beautiful.

Her breasts were against his chest as she watched him swallow the cognac. "I cannot decide if you remind me of a thug dressed like a cleric . . . more robust than most of course . . . Just cannot decide if churching tempered the lout . . . or the hood strengthened the prelate."

She slid to her knees in front of him. His hand was rough

and leathery, callused on fingers and palms. The ring was large and hard against her mouth. After she kissed it, her hand undid his suit jacket. Reverently or irreverently, depending on how one looks at it, she pulled his zipper down and went exploring within the clerical black. The gabardine didn't hamper her, and the beast wanted out. Very quickly, she had freed what she wanted. Taking half a mouthful of the superior cognac, putting the tumbler aside on the rug, she took Arthur Danley into her mouth.

The cognac grew salty. She felt her bra snap and fall to either side. He must have put his brandy down for two large violent hands grabbed her breasts and drew them out of her blouse. They rubbed against the roughness of his trousers. She was swallowing oceans, licking the spit of the land for more. Lick, her tongue found the groove. Curl, lick, loop, the pressure on her breasts grew tremendous. She felt a great shudder. The roots of her hair felt as if they were being pulled from her scalp.

Mir, as if holding onto a mountain, put her arms around the strong thighs. Glued to him, taking as much of him into her mouth as she could, she held the mountain that was struck by lightning while it shook.

His labored breathing returned part way to normal. He pulled her up, his big hand sliding under the black skirt and curving around back inside her panties. The ring finger caught; they heard the silky fabric tear.

"You won'd need these," Arthur Danley murmured. He ripped the panties off completely, and flung them into the corner. "Now, my dear, if you still want to make that confession I'll be very glad to hear it." He lifted her up. One finger up her ass, he carried her back to his room.

Sleepily, she threw the down comforter off her body; the heat was incredible. She imagined she could see the waves rising from her torso into the coolness of the room. Patting the sheet at her side, she realized she was alone in the bed even as she heard the voices.

A man, not Arthur, was speaking in a decidedly irritated, strangely nasal voice. "Hell, Art, I didn't expect the guy to pull that. He moved from a sitting position *so* fast! Never saw anything like it.

"When I woke up, I got myself over to Metropolitan and had it taken care of. Told the doc my girl beat me up and I didn't want to press charges."

There was a long silence then she heard Arthur's voice. "Recognize him?"

"No. But if I ever see him again I will, moved like a cat."

"You'd better go home and get some rest."

"No. Brincussi's on patrol, I think I should see Savior, get it over with tonight. I wanted you to come with me."

"Afraid of the old guy?" There was no answer. Now Arthur sounded annoyed. "Couldn't it wait 'til daylight?"

"Hey man, someone's on your tail. He's gonna want to see you anyway. Why not come with me and get it over with. He should know about it. Maybe he can lift them."

Mir lay with her eyes closed, breathing evenly, as Arthur came into the bedroom, went to the wall of closets, and fumbled in the dark with his clothes. She heard him pick his shoes up and come over to the side of the bed where he stood for a good minute looking down at her. Then he bent and pulled the comforter slowly up over her nakedness.

Grateful now for the warmth of the comforter, she lay listening to the garage door open, the powerful engine purr its

161

way onto the pre-dawn streets. Someone on guard had encountered a prowler. Someone had replaced him. Brancussi was on prowl now watching the place. Both inside and out?, she wondered.

The heavy curtains were drawn; she didn't touch the light-switch. Recalling the layout, she rose and walked to the farthest closet, the one where Arthur's clerical black hung. The cassocks were too big and too long, but a naked, cold woman in need of a robe cannot be choosy.

She felt like a nun in a choir habit with the sleeves hanging down past her wrists, or like Dopey, the seventh dwarf. If she encountered this Brancussi character, she would say she was on the way to the bathroom.

The hall was dimly lit and very quiet. The large centrally placed room where Arthur had torn her panties and thrown them in a corner was dark. She glanced in as she passed along to the room where she left her case.

She didn't turn on the light there either. Finding the case on the bureau where she'd left it, she searched through it for her mini mag lite from L. L. Bean. On second thought, she pulled the folder out of the bottom. It held the first draft of the final chapter of the Valery article. She carried it everywhere re-reading, putting in finishing touches . . . She'd brought it down this evening more out of habit than anything else.

The flashlight was a necessity. Never again would she be caught in a city power outtage without a light. Holding the skirts of the cassock up, knowing there was no one else within the apartment, she decided to go back to Arthur's room. She'd seen a reading light on a pull-down suspension cord over his side of the bed.

But without discussing it with herself at all, she passed his open door and walked toward the last closed door in the corridor. Spending the night in strange surrounding? Rule 1: Familiarize yourself!

Placing the folder on the rug by her bare toes, she reached for the door knob, the long sleeves of heavy fabric falling over her fingers. It opened. The room seemed to be a reading room or library. The bright tiny beam illuminated a pile of books by a Lazy-boy. The slick cover of *Patriot Games* by Tom Clancy shone. Beside it, *Selous Scouts—Top Secret War* by Lt. Col. Reid Daly and *Basic Stickfighting for Combat*. Mir walked slowly over to a table covered with newspapers and magazines. *Secrets of Underground Organizations* was half buried under *Soldiers of Fortune* magazine and a copy of *Knife Self Defense for Combat*. An illustrated guide to *Modern Elite Forces* had a heavy glass ashtray sitting on it.

Bookcases along the far wall . . . she let the light play along the spines. *Los Banos Raid. The Specialist* by Gayle Rivers. The *U.S. Armed Forces Survival Manual. Inevitable Revolution* by Walter LeFeber. *Get Tough, The Special Forces Physical Conditioning Program* by Tom Fitzgerald. MaoTseTung on *Guerilla Warfare. Military Incompetence,* Richard A. Gabriel and *The Art of War* by Sun Tzu. *Military Small Arms of the Twentieth Century,* and *The Vietnam Weapons Handbook. Survivors* by Zalin Grant. *Into Laos* . . . the titles went on. A veritable military school library.

Not exactly church material, she thought, letting the beam of light shine on her toes. Absentmindedly, she flexed her bare feet; there was no pile under them here. Everywhere the rugs had been soft and deep except . . . right . . . here. Mir shone the mini lite back on the wall, the wall of books. There was a door behind this section; she was sure of it. Back over the books her fingers went, carefully and slowly. Behind the *U.S. Army's Special Forces Medical Handbook* she found the button. Startled, she stepped back as the bookshelf swung in away from her.

She purposefully draped the sleeves over her hands now, making sure she touched nothing as she entered the large walk-in closet.

A gun rack ran the width and length of the room. Polished wood and burnished steel, she surveyed the extent of it. Six shiny Heckler Kochs rested their new barrels against the maple directly in front of her. Then, two assault rifles. She bent nearer and peered at the heavy Fabric Nationals. Belgium make? She seemed to recall they were used mainly by the United Kingdom Countries. There were three AUGs, three Russian AK-47's, six M-16's.

A shelf underneath was stacked with sealed canisters. Next to these watertight cans lay a long, wooden box with Chinese characters on it. Boxes of 7.62 thirty caliber NATO rounds were piled on the other side of the metal canisters.

Mir shone light on the far wall, then walked up to it. She'd never seen the Israeli design UZI outside of the movies. Twelve UZI submachine guns rested in their wooden collars beside six Heckler Kochs, boxes of nine millimeter shells stacked up over head. Below the subs, half a dozen colt automatics lay on soft green material, two 357 magnums, King Cobra stamped on their barrels, lay beside four government issue Delta Elites.

Curiously, she looked at the next four. She'd read about these only recently in a small weapons manual that came through the publishing firm. Made of space age polymers the blurb had spouted, the Glock 17, weighing less than twenty-four ounces, would be the harbinger of a whole new era in handgun manufacturing. Developed for the Austrian military, adopted by NATO. It takes a NATO round then, she thought.

It was a fucking arsenal! The light from the flashlight swung to a shelf she hadn't noticed behind the wooden box with the Chinese characters. They weren't beer cans! They stood like empty soldiers at a party except they were not empty. Concussion grenades.

She hadn't touched a thing. God, Arthur must not suspect she had been in here. Firmly, she closed the door behind her with the sleeve over her fingers, the shelves slid into place. Quickly, she walked through the library without dislodging any of the books, again, closing the door carefully. Stooping, she picked up her Valery article and returned to his bed to think.

There was no sleeping. She sat upright in the middle of the bed, her mind churning. When Arthur returned, she wanted him to find the woman he left. What then to do with the woman who had just found Bluebeard's den? Put her out to pasture for the remainder of the night came the mocking chorus.

A hot shower would help. And lights. Brancussi who knew she was here would know she was awake. Good. Reaching up, she pulled the reading light on over the bed.

An hour later, hearing the garage door open, feeling the low, vibratory silent running of the powerful engine, she was ready.

Arthur Danley, returning alone, was met by a short, wiry man in black. "All quiet. No further sign of that guy. Your lady-friend woke about an hour ago, showered, made herself something to eat." The man searched Arthur's face greedily, but was not rewarded. He gave a husky laugh. "Well, have fun."

He stood quietly at the door of his room taking in the sight of her. She sat cross-legged in the middle of his bed with her back to him. Her hair under the light and over the black of his cassock was suddenly deep red. She'd rolled the cassock sleeves and pulled the skirt for freedom of movement, up above her naked thighs. The bed was littered with papers.

A plate holding the remnants of a roll lay on top the papers and a brandy snifter, half full, sat atop the box of Hava Yorcas. She was bent over the papers in her hand, chewing on a pencil. He swallowed. She heard.

"Arthur!" She hadn't buttoned the front of the cassock and as she turned, her right breast fell out. "Do you always go out in the middle of the night to work?"

"Do you always feel like writing after jumping into bed with a guy?"

She patted an area of cleared sheet to the side of her, "Come. Come give me an opinion. I've been going over the Valery article. What do you think he means by this? 'Nothing alters or transfigures us more profoundly than the struggle against those of our powers that have turned against us.'" He ran his fingers like a comb through her hair, scooping it to the top of her head. Leaning across him for a sheet of heavily red-penciled script, she seemed unaware that her left breast had come clear.

Fingering the small, black buttons she said simply, "It's not organized, just look at this! Oh, by the way, I hope you don't mind my borrowing your priestly robe. I was cold when I

166

woke." She was thoughtful again, "You know, P. V. said he needed three eunuch slaves, intelligent, and infinitely compliant, one to read his papers, one to tell him he understood, and the last, a secretary stenographer." She took a deep breath. The nipples bobbed.

"You're a tease. You know that, don't you."

She looked into the fire in his eyes and smiled. "It's the little girl playing hide and seek again with the neighborhood boy in the dark cellar."

He pressed a pink nipple between a thumb and forefinger, "What happened when he caught you?"

"He never did."

Twisting to the side to retrieve something, her nipple pulled out from between his fingers. She bent across, her loose breasts whispering on his arm. The curly golden hairs lay down for the body of the breasts going after the papers, drifting softly to the floor. The hairs, disturbed, pushed hither and thither . . .

His breath came heavy and fast. Two brawny arms pulled the all too large cassock down off her shoulders. Standing her, holding her under the arms, he shook her out of it.

Putting a hand out, he grabbed the comforter and flipped it. The comforter whirled like pizza dough in mid-air. It flew so quickly that the piece of roll stayed on its plate. The brandy was a liquid curtain hurrying to catch up with its departing bowl, unsuccessfully, for when the snifter landed, upright, all but a half an inch had departed. Lazily, papers fluttered and settled across the room.

She laughed, watching the topaz liquid slosh around in the glass. "You couldn't do that again if you tried."

"Probably not," he grinned, pulled off his dark sweater and jeans with one hand and grabbed her back against him. One hand successfully took up the whole of both breasts, the other thrust roughly between her legs. .

He withdrew a lubricious hand, making the sign of the cross before anointing her forehead.

"There are special blessings for women. From time immemorial they seem to have been in need of them . . . according to the powers that be, that is . . ." It was the ecclestiac speaking, the Bishop . . . possible future Cardinal. His fingers trailed langorously down her cheek, her neck.

He pushed deep into her with his hand, brought his dripping fingers to her lips. "Taste!" Her smell came to her on his hands. His wet fingers probed her mouth. Sucking opened sluice gates in her pelvis, flooding her upper thighs.

Thirty years within the confessional had taught him a thing or two . . . or was it the expert in tactical warfare? Her breasts were fondled tenderly, crossed with the sign and oiled. He progressed to her belly, thighs, knees . . . feet. The candles were all lit on the altar . . .

"Now for those lovely orifices." There was a requisite priestly gravity to the tone of his voice.

Daylight was seeping around the corners of the drapes,

"It's going to be a busy day."

"You said you had to leave town?"

"Yeah, gotta make an eleven a.m. flight. Couple of things I should do before that too." His breath forced out in a tidal wave.

"You never told me what you thought of the Valery quote."

"I agree with him, seen it happen."

"You actually heard me, I don't believe it. You were not completely smitten by my state of dishabille," she smiled teasingly. Then, "Have any of your powers turned against you?"

"Nope." He was curling her sticky pubic hair into spirals and peaks. "And as far as the other goes . . . I've never had the slightest need of a eunuch.

"Will I see you when I get back?" he asked. She looked suddenly thoughtful. When she didn't answer: "Well?"

Mir sat up then and swung herself around, straddling his narrow pelvis. She relaxed her weight. Gazing at the bulk of him lying back against the pillows she searched his face, "I think so."

"OK. That's good enough for now."

Chapter Fifteen

The graveyard shift at police headquarters was busy making its way home. Walt Bathesday watched Eli. Seldom was he seen here this early—he liked to work out in the morning—and never looking so rumpled. He appeared to have slept in his overcoat.

Long legs stretched out across the desk-top, chair tilted backwards, head cocked at a neck-breaking angle on the three quarters file. Lost in thought, oblivious of the hubbub, every sixty seconds he moved a bead on the abacus.

Bath was as interested in the ancient counting device as Eli's unkempt state. A change was in the wind. For months the abacus rested in the drawer. When it came forth and Eli sat fingering the beads like a senile nun, it did not mean change was upcoming that very day, but it sure was imminent.

So, Walt Bathesday was sitting quietly waiting.

"Tried to reach you last night," Bath said.

"Had to go to the City."

He couldn't translate the expression on his face, couldn't see it. So he wasn't with her. The locker room tab had it that Eli and Marion Rasille were a sudden twosome. A hot twosome. Bath hoped it was true; Ms. Rasille was quite a looker. And Eli, well, he had dropped ten years.

"Had coffee at Mom's when I got back, then came here."

"I checked out Maysenrod," Bath said. "Got his fingers in more pies than you'd find at a pie-eating contest. Old guy, he's been around. Over eighty now. He was a colonel in Special Forces back when Arthur Danley was in Korea. Money! Lots of it! He doesn't deal the big D, but I'd say he comes right close. He will sell to developing nations anything they need to get developed. They need it, he's got it."

"Munitions?"

"Yup."

Eli moved another bead. "I trailed Danley last night."

"You trailed the bishop?"

"He drove a car registered to Maysenrod. Went into a house owned by Maysenrod. A house by the way, that is under some very elite surveillance." Eli took a deep breath. "His Reverence did not act like a bishop."

There was a long silence. "You look godawful."

"Thanks." Eli did not look particularly stung.

"Maybe this will help you feel better. Our contact in Laos tells us that an elderly female, a staunch Party member, was buried last week without a hand. Since she hasn't had a hand for two years and no one knows how she lost it, it wasn't considered momentous. The lady was not liked. Everyone on both sides was glad she had finally passed away. She was 78.

"Our Laotian also had a kernel of interest. He says twenty years ago some CIA types and a priest made a flying leap through their country looking for a downed flyer. There was a lot of fire power in the group, that's how he remembers it.

The guy in charge was a tough bastard and the priest, a tall, thin, nervous type. He heard they never found him, the pilot. One last nugget." You could see Bath savoring this morsel. "A couple of months ago in Southwest Cambodia, a local Khmer Rouge leader's brother, thirty-three years old, crafty little zealot, turned up missing a foot. He disappeared for a day and a half. They thought he had a woman stashed somewhere. When his comrades found him he was laughing his head off. Coked-out. He told them a bad dream about the CIA. They think he stepped on a mine, but that wouldn't explain the fact that his stump was bandaged all neat and clean."

Eli forced air through his lips. "Good work!" He was grinning. They watched John Fay amble toward them, hands thrust deep in his pockets, with his frequent hangdog look. He was having trouble with Nancy. They shook their heads.

When he sat down, Bath growled at him, "Why in blazes don't you marry her!"

Fay looked sheepish and scowled. They brought him up to date and watched the eyebrows go up, the alert expression return. Bath, watching the transformation, swore anew he was never going to get too involved with any woman. They were good for maybe one or two things. Best to take them home then, where they belonged, leave a guy his peace.

"John, I need a door to door around Hilary's. You may have to go farther. Let's see if anyone saw Elias leave the rectory that Tuesday. We've got to find them."

Eli was musing to himself then, "So, old clawhand lived at least two years after she stopped breathing and was given that shot of epinephrine. Find out where she was living when she lost the hand. Can we place Elias there during his yearly visit?

"We have to know exactly where Elias went this year. Can we fit him with the loss of the henchman's foot? On second thought," he glanced at the wall clock, "I could see to the good father this morning."

"You should go home and go to bed."

"Later. Things are changing. You have to keep on the move-ment with change, or the resulting dilemma is incompre-hensible." He stood up, and standing, his dishevelment looked like dilemma enough. The abacus disappeared into the desk drawer.

Unawareness of one's feet is the mark of shoes that fit. Un-awareness of right and wrong is the mark of a mind at ease. Father Elias' shoes fit, Eli thought, watching the priest walk away. Often people blurt out the truth. It hasn't a thing to do with whether you are doing a good job tightening the rope. Their guilt gets to them; they need to confess.

Elias was not riddled with guilt. He was going back to the rectory to build a second kitchen cabinet. Cool as cold celery, he told Eli where he was in Southwestern Cambodia eight weeks ago and then, if that was all, he had work to do, turned and walked away.

After talking with Father Elias, he had rung the monastery door bell on impulse and asked for Sister Damian. "It's me, myself," her cheerful, low voice answered at the turn. They could talk as long as he didn't mind being interrupted. She would have to answer the phone and buzzer when they rang.

They met in the speakroom. "I was searching through the archives for information," she gestured toward the photos, "and came across those." She shuddered, remembering. "We passed them through community just as we did when they ini-tially came in the mails. No one said a word. You know war is hell," she finished lamely, "but you don't really know. We have accumulated this collection over a period of twenty years.

"Each one arrived with a heartbreaking appeal for prayers, usually for a POW or someone missing in action. As I said, we looked at them again after recreation last night. I am sure they've burned fresh into each sister's soul.

Eli felt calmer sitting there than he had in twenty-four hours. Her brow was smooth. A dimple laughed in her cheek when he teased her about the "it's me, myself."

"I was glad to hear your voice. Father Elias had just left. We talked." The look she gave him was both expressionless and hopeful.

"Sister, I'd like to keep these for awhile if I may?" "Of course." He was beginning to look like the dime novel detective, Sister Damian thought. "Detective, you look like you could use some coffee."

"If I drink any more I'll twang."

She laughed. "Tough night?"

"Wasn't easy Sister."

"Tea then."

He sat looking at the pictures while she was off making it; they were not nice viewing.

Sister Damian leafed through the clippings in a makeshift scrapbook when she returned. "Maybe you should have these as well . . . No . . . I can't do that, maybe you could, well, go through them? You see I've promised them to someone who is going to be writing about our congregation." Damian said, almost talking to herself, "I was dubious about the article, but it has been a help to go through these again. They throw some light."

"Do you recognize anyone in the photos, Sister?"

She seemed to have pondered this already. "I would say, cautiously, no. Pain disfigures though, enormously. Something about . . ." She faltered. "Those cages were ghastly!" She swallowed hard. "A fleeting forgotten recognition, Detective, gone before it came. I don't know, it was puzzling to me. I may have internalized the torture, seen myself."

"Where does it shine, Sister?"

"What?"

"The light."

"Oh. Well, on our order, this community of sisters. And on the changes that have taken place. A provocative dilemma comes in the guise of a one-legged man." She leaned forward and touched the grillwork as if assuring herself of its reality. "He always had the other leg, you know, he just never used it."

"You're particularly enigmatic this morning, Sister."

"Am I? Well, I only meant that . . . I've been spending a lot of time in the basement. Oh Lord!" She started chuckling. The laughter made her rock back and forth. As she rocked, the laughter increased in volume. At this point, she looked up at Detective Eli Janah and pointed her finger at him. "You look godawful!"

"I do, don't I?" Eli Janah's face broke into a ripple of laugh lines, and he threw back his head and howled.

In between gasps, she said, "You look the way they describe detectives in murder mysteries. See, this may be one of your real selves that has just out." A growl of laughter shook him. She continued, "I like the other one, don't get me wrong. But I thought he was kinda neat."

"Too neat for a detective?" His eyes were teasing.

"No, I guess not." She smiled at him. He caught the glitter in her eyes of the unshed tears, the tears that had turned to laughter.

175

"Well!" There was a business-as-usual shade to her chin although the smile refused to leave. "If you're in the mood and ye have the time, you're quite welcome to stay and look through this stuff. I brought four crates up from the basement. They'll not fit in the drawer; I'll pass them out at the turn."

Eli, realizing that things were going well with very little planning on his part, agreed. There was a bench in the room, and he carried the crates in from the front turn and lay them side by side on this. Taking off his suit jacket, rolling up his sleeves, he pulled the table and chair within easy reach and began sorting the ingredients of the wooden boxes.

Sister Damian left to answer the front doorbell. He caught something about a key to the chapel. Then a phone rang and there were voices and the whole thing washed out like background noise along with bells and a half hours chanting from the sisters' wing of the chapel.

What he had before him within two hours was evidence of a large scale operation in Southeast Asia. An operation of this size could hide any number of things. The late Monsignor O'Reilly had been fundamental to its functioning.

Lists of contacts, schedules for airlifting, ferry-boat captains, money paid out from donations and special collections, national health officials, housing representatives, immigration officials, Red Cross, philanthropic organizations. The names of hundreds of children, age, origin, place of disembarkment, whether or not there were siblings or other members of the family in the States. All was written in a neat woman's hand.

At noon he sat back and listened to the bells in the tower ring the three and three and three and did not know it was the Angelus.

No Sephiroth rose and fell between the wet, dark monastery

176

and the wall of the enclosure. The tree that represents the dynamic underlying reality of the world of sense was being slowly surface-coated, a habit of cloaking in the way of hemlock and pine. Turgid rain hit the windows and froze. The tops of the cloister garden gradually faded from view.

He hadn't heard Sister Damian. Leaning back against the door, she stood very still watching him from her side of the speakroom. "I suspect I'll not be seeing much of you from now on, Detective Janah." Eli felt warmth and calm wash over him.

"I suspect not, Sister."

He pointed to the piles of papers and books before him. "This has been very helpful. May I make a suggestion?"

"Of course."

"Put it away. Better still, burn it. Whatever you do, don't make it accessible to the public just yet. You say someone is writing about the Congregation? If I were you, I would refrain from extending him this material."

"Her."

"No matter."

Eli didn't for one moment think that the sisters knew of covert operations within the confines of their charity. Sister Damian gave him a long, hard look. "Maybe that's why the Lord sent you this morning, Detective. I'll do what you advise." He never asked her which piece of advice she chose for her course of action. "I came in to see if you would also like something to eat?"

"Thanks." he shook his head in the negative and patted his flat abdomen. "Notice how quiet it is."

The long, relaxed figure of the recumbent man. The tall erect nun in her grey habit. Frozen in place. Sleet fitting itself into the window mosaic made the only sound. An artist with an eye to angles and planes, would see the exact amount of rotation required to bring one figure into coincidence with the other. The frank grey eyes of the nun and the eyes of the soon-to-be Inspector held their common knowledge lightly.

John Fay was waiting outside Eli's apartment in his car. "Coming up?"

Fay nodded. "Just for a few minutes though. Nancy and I are going for the license this afternoon."

Eli grinned and slapped him on the shoulder. "Way to go, man! Two people who make each other as miserable as you two have some fate to work out."

Fay, sitting at the kitchen table, said no to coffee. "Jittery enough." But he was smiling. "I had a real stroke of luck this morning. Kinda take it as an omen. The muffler fell off my wreck on Pine Street, I was dragging the tail pipe. To make a long story short, I clattered into Clancy's Garage to have him wire it up until I can get time to take it in. He doesn't think much of guys who misuse their cars.

"St. Hilary's has a sedan, an '84 black Chevy. It had a couple of teeth missing on the fly wheel. Made a hell of a noise but it usually caught . . . if you cranked the starter enough. Clancy asked them not to use it, and he tabled all other jobs to get it in the bay on the eighth.

"Well, he was out with the tow, retrieving old Mrs. Jacobs from a ditch when he saw Father Elias drive that car in the direction of the Annunciation at one-thirty on the seventh. He was pissed. Unnecessary abuse of a car, he calls it. He never said anything to the fathers, but he charged them extra for the work."

"He's sure it was Father Elias?"

"Positive."

Eliaphus Daniel Janah let the hot water beat on his head and shoulders. Five seconds after throwing himself on his bed, he was asleep.

Chapter Sixteen

The moment of combustion is pure silence. Eli's face was expressionless. Absorbed, he reached out and rearranged the photographs. There were nineteen. He had been examining them with diligence since he woke.

Reverently, he laid one photo beside another and then another beside that . . . then another . . . until he had a separate grouping of seven on his left. Carefully, he went over the remaining eleven with the magnifying glass. Who had taken them?

If forgetting is absolute solace and absolute injustice as Kundera says, then someone holding a camera decided there was to be no forgetting. They passed judgment.

He held one closer to the light. The young GI's face was almost washed out in the blaze of uncamouflaged pain. In fact, his entire naked body glowed with a pallid light. The old woman sawing away on him couldn't have been more delineated if she had been in a line-up; you could clearly make out the mole on her lip. The Mark 4 survival knife that cut through the man's body part was distinctly identifiable. The hand that stretched his flesh for the serrated edge, looked like the claw of an eagle.

In another, a small Asian, barely more than a boy, kicked a pulpy mass. Only when he had identified the small, round hanging object as an eye, waiting like an egg for the next thrust of the boot, did he realize the mass had been a man's face.

In eleven of the photographs, the camera sight focused on the torturer. Despite the baggy pajamas, two were definitely female. He was looking at a picture of 'clawhand' in her mid or late sixties.

He had not been positive that the seven he had placed to one side were of one and the same man. At least initially. At first, only two surprised him with their likenesses.

A young uniformed American was being hoisted above a crowd of angry villagers in a four-foot square cage. He must have been very tall, his knees were jutting up on either side of his face.

The second was a close-up of his face. The photo looked like a picture of Father Elias.

In the third photograph, the man's face had altered appreciably. He had been stripped naked. Two men were jabbing him with long poles. He hung above them in a kind of village square. He seemed to be trying to avoid the thrusts, but there was no place he could go. Eli winced at the position of one of the poles. The face of the man puncturing the caged man's rectum was very clear.

There were four more photos, three of him still caged. There was a definite time sequence. But Eli could not tell how many years had intervened between the caging of the captured, downed flyer and the picture of the emaciated skeleton that did not bother to look through the bars of the cage.

The resemblance to Father Elias had faded. Only the broad

brow and a hint at the corner of the eyes retained a slight familial likeness.

What hair he had was white and was distributed in a most unusual pattern across his head. It took Eli some minutes before he realized it must have been pulled out in clumps. There was a far-away vacant stare in the eyes of the life form in the cage as if the soul had spirited the mind away.

The legs, imprisoned for so long in their scrunched-up position, looked like gnarled tree limbs.

The last picture was a puzzle until Eli got his bearings. A naked human form, skin taut over a gaunt skull, lay on its back on the bare dirt like an upended beetle, the limbs grotesquely twisted like antlers in the air.

Eli glanced out the window. A drop in temperature had changed the icy drizzle to flakes floating lazily in the street light. He knew what Sister Damian had known when she suggested he borrow the photographs. He knew why.

It gave him no satisfaction. The pervasive dis-ease that he did feel finally drove him away from the table into the practice room. Spreading the mats on the bare floor, he stripped and quickly worked up a sweat. Toweling himself, he did not leave the room.

Sitting on the mat wrapped up in the oversized towel, he thought of the I Ching's insistence on change . . . of paying attention to transitions.

He had followed a wire, found it was faulty. Now it was his job; no, his duty, to see it was re-placed. It did not matter that that particular wire began to look like the soundest part of the system. No, that did not matter at all.

The larger warp was of no consequence, outside his realm

of concern. Anyway, he had no proof. Suppositions against a formidable enemy—he laughed thinking what an illusion that would be.

The Chinese have a saying that calls upon a man to walk on both legs. Was he thinking of retirement? No. Then he had a few years. Who knows what a vigilant man can do in a few years. He had a lot to learn about using two or more faculties instead of one. He had a lot to learn about walking on two legs.

Standing, he kicked the towel away and dropped his body into 'beginning stance.' Yin was the fleeting stillness of 'grasp birds tail.' Where the yang energy took over was impossible to tell. Flowing into the concluding harmony of 'ward off left' subtly indivisible from form. Tai Chi Chuan, activity—quiescence.

There was a world of difference in his inner being when he finished. Before he showered, he picked up the phone and told Walt Bath to get a search warrant for St. Hilary's rectory.

"I know it's Friday, Walt," he said calmly, "but try Debittle, he won't mind. You and John wait 'til morning. Around six or six-thirty Father Elias starts for the Annunciation to say Mass. Find me those instruments. I'll be in the monastery church; bring them to me." He listened for a few minutes. "I've no doubt you'll find them."

When he came from the shower, the clock on the shelf over the yarrow stalks read 9:10. A look out the window told him what his ears had told him, there had been a steady accumulation of snow. This time when he asked information for Mirari's number, he got a listing.

He held the phone while it rang. On the sixth ring, she

183

caught up the receiver, her voice groggy. "Mir, it's Eli." There was a silence that did not bode well. Then he realized she was making an effort to wake completely.

"Eli? Oh, how are you?"

"I woke you, I'm sorry."

"No, no, I hadn't actually gone to bed, I fell asleep in front of the fire."

"One of the kids told me you were back in the house . . . I tried to call . . ."

"I just got around to having the phone connected . . . but of course you already know that if you tried to call."

He felt suddenly shy. "How are you?" He wanted to see her very much . . . too much.

"Eli, this is ridiculous, this phone business, why don't you come up? Bring some Tom and Jerry's? Vanilla. I'll put another log on the fire."

The Friday night traffic was fierce, despite—or maybe because of—the snow. By the time he got the ice cream and drove the Nissan up the unplowed driveway, it was 10:15.

"You're probably getting up early," he said wanting to kick himself as soon as it was out. He was always apologizing for breathing with Mir. It made him furious and her also. At least it had at one time. She didn't seem to notice now, but was busy digging into the tub of vanilla with a big stainless steel spoon.

"You're having some, right?"

"Right."

He followed her through the house to the fire. Neither spoke. Eli settled himself in the lazy-boy, Mir flopped among her pillows on the hearth. They ate the ice cream in companionable silence.

Mir spoke first, "I want to ask how you are, but I don't want the truth, the whole truth and nothing but the truth so help me God."

He smiled at her across the room, "I know."

Apologetically then, "I like the space, Eli; I can breathe." The tone begged him to understand. He lay the empty bowl on the rug and relaxed his lanky frame back in the chair so that his feet shot up.

"Marriage is just too much enforced intimacy, isn't it?" He searched her face. She nodded. "We'll keep it light then. We could talk about the kids."

She grinned devilishly down at her empty bowl. "I'd rather hear what you're doing."

"Wrapping up a case."

"Really?"

"Yes."

"Are you glad to be finished?"

He didn't answer right away. "Yes and no. I guess I found out more than I wanted to know."

"Yes!" Mir drew a deep breath remembering the other night and let it out with the exclamation.

He looked at her in surprise. "You know what I mean?" She nodded.

Though the grey had advanced since she'd seen him last, he looked surprisingly young and vulnerable. She remembered the first time they'd met. How she had loved the look of him!

He was reading the look on her face. She sat with her spoon poised half way to her mouth watching him with wide eyes. The look in her eyes, the way her face flushed with the warmth of the fire, belied what she had just said about intimacy. He never moved on Mir the way he would another woman. After

185

all, she was the mother of his children. He had too much respect for her. But, something was different tonight. She wasn't
his wife. The kids weren't here. A generous breasted woman
with a wild mass of hair and long, very good legs, was giving
him a very steady look from across the rug.

Eli Janah thought of the pictures back on his kitchen table.
He thought of the next morning. He stared at the fire. Then
rising, he crossed to her, knelt down and started undoing the
buttons on the white linen caftan. Mir lay back upon the larg-
est of the pillows with a sigh.

"You've changed," she said in a very soft voice. He undid
another button, looked at her teasingly, questioningly,

"Yes?"

She nodded. When he drew her to him, the caftan fell down
off her shoulders.

Reverend Mother Michaels looked over the community
from her choir stall at the rear of the church. No one was leaving. They had finished the recitation of Matins and Lauds, the
first hour of the daily Office traditionally sung in the late evening of the previous day and the entire community had remained kneeling.

In recent months at least a dozen sisters genuflected and left
before the lights went out for the Friday night discipline. She
felt a curious catch in her throat. She'd give them another minute.

Sister Damian's unprecedented plea for prayers at supper
had startled the community. It was unlike Damian to get so
emotional. Michaels intuited the investigation was at an end.
You would think she'd turned in the insane individual who had
carried out the terrible vengeance. After she spoke, she barely

touched her food. Michaels looking now around the church could find no other reasonable explanation.

She motioned to Sister Anne to throw the lights. It was perfectly quiet, the calm night and the softly falling snow made their own enclosure. Michaels began the psalm, "Misere mei, Deus . . ." to the rustling of many skirts.

Such great pain pierced her at the thought of those hands and feet, that she never felt the tiny knots cut into her skin.

Wash me from mine iniquity, cleanse me from my sin. Against Thee only have I sinned and done evil before Thee. Thou shalt sprinkle me with hyssop and I shall be cleansed. Thou shalt wash me and I shall be made whiter than snow. Turn away thy face from my sins. Create in me a clean heart. Cast me not away from Thy face . . . the voices of the nuns begged for one of their own.

Restore unto me the joy of Thy salvation . . . Silence then blanketed the little church. Mother Michaels waited a discreet while before turning on the small choir light by her kneeler and then made the signal for the community to file out to their cells.

If the elderly man wrapped in his muffler thought anything of running into the tall detective at the monastery church at 6:45 a.m., he didn't indicate this.

"Mornin'." His eyes rose briefly, then dove as he hurried past. Eli followed him in.

Sitting in a pew by the door, he watched a very short altar boy wave a very long pole with a little flame on the end at the high altar candles. The tiny fire spun around and around like an undecided bee. Eli grinned. You couldn't see the boy's face, but every muscle in his body showed the tension and determination as his hands gripped and tried to steady the pole. Finally, the flame kissed the wick lightly in passing. It caught.

His shoulders straightened, he marched to the center, genuflected, stumbled on his robe getting up, and lurched crazily to the other side to begin all over again.

Lights went off and another set came on behind the curtained window of the cloister. A pipe struck a key and the voices of the nuns began the Ave Maria Stella.

As the parishioners returned from communion, John Fay eased along the pew from the other end and sat down beside Eli. "It's a beautiful set." He passed a heavy leather case across to Eli. Mrs. Berens had hidden it away among her things . . . her flannel nightgowns to be exact."

Eli's eyebrows arched. "She knows a lot more than she'll say."

"Walt's in the car. What do you want us to do?"

"Wait. In the car."

"I've been expecting you, Detective Janah." Eli moved along the bench to give Father Elias room. The priest had thrown all the light switches about the altar except the one glancing on the angel of the Annunciation. He had been studying it during the service, but until the church was thrown in semi-darkness, the relief wasn't enough to be sure.

Now he knew, and he felt a curious elation at seeing it again. It was a good imitation of the four foot high Venetian marble he'd seen in the Cloisters some years back. "Istrian. Very beautiful, isn't it?" Elias watched him.

"15th centurion loan for the celebration of the founding of the Congregation."

"It's the real thing?"

"Yes."

"I saw it years ago. Couldn't get my feet to continue past it for the longest time." Father Elias nodded. He glanced at his case resting lightly on Eli's knees. Eli saw the movement of the priest's eyes. "I didn't really need them, but I wanted to see them," he explained. "Do you want to tell me about it?"

Father Elias looked across the darkened church to the sanctuary and sighed, "Yes. It's time." The lights went out within the cloister. The two men heard a click and a great rustling as the community genuflected and began to leave to go about their daily tasks. The priest waited until all was silent behind the grill.

"The Milanesians call it Mana, Detective. The Sioux, Wakanda. The Iroquois, Orenda. The Algonquin, Manitou. Our evil is a hidden indwelling that can give us great power. Hidden as it is, it's neutral, it can discharge favorably or unfavorably." There was a forcefulness in the voice, "I discovered that a hunt can enable a man to acquire a great Mana."

"Your brother did not die in 1965 or in 1967."

"No," Elias said simply. He looked Eli in the eyes, "He didn't die then. "It was a mess over there," he sighed. "For a long time the jets were only allowed to fly through the tree tops and scare the hell out of the monkeys. Ground units could not talk directly to the fighter units; their radios didn't mesh. Ground forces had to radio their coordinates to the helicopters who in turn radioed the planes. Batteries went out on the radios. No one knew if they were going to last one hour or three days.

"Our guys killed each other. They killed the monkeys. They had so many damn rules of engagement up until March 1965 . . . Politicians called it displaying a presence . . .

"Tim was flying cover for Marine Advisory Teams, MDTAs and protecting long range re-con patrols. They were told to fly low over the Vietcong, scare them off. Those F-4B Phantoms make awesome noise!

"He was on the first deep probe past the Chu Lai enclave South of Da Nang. It was Vietcong country. From what I've gleaned, he was allowed to fire that day." He looked aside at Eli. "Johnson finally allowed direct combat operations between the United States and communist forces in South Vietnam."

Father Elias' voice was low, "Did you know that we dropped two and a half times the tonnage of bombs on Vietnam that we dropped in World war II? Tim crashed south of Da Nang near Tam Ky. He was twenty-eight years old.

"In 1967, I heard he was alive. Official channels said he was dead. But at that time, someone approached me, someone very unofficial, and convinced me he was alive. The Vietcong had taken him back into Laos."

"You went over and tried to get him out."

Elias wrung his hands, "I had to try."

"How long did he live in that cage?"

A sob tore itself from the man's breast beside him. Eli heard him swallow hard, straighten his shoulders. "Ten years. They made an example of him.

"They kept moving him. No matter how fast we went in, how hard we worked at grabbing him . . . we were always a day, an hour, forty minutes too late."

"O'Reilly had connections?"

"Yes."

"Danley?"

Father Elias' voice was very firm, "No. O'Reilly was enough, with a score of mercenaries and mystagogues." He shook his head, remembering. "We caught up with him when they had no more use for him."

"He was still alive?"

"Yes."

"You killed him," Eli's tone was decisive.

A groan came from the throat of the man sitting beside him. "I couldn't pull the trigger . . . as bad as he was, I couldn't pull the trigger. One of the guys. I held him . . ." He couldn't finish.

The priest stared at the small, red sanctuary light flickering on the main altar. "I started hunting with O'Reilly's help. He had contacts, God, he had contacts. I rode a hundred six-bys those years, if I rode one." He felt Eli's look. "Marine Corps trucks." A smug smile came over his face, "They'll never know how much their propaganda helped me."

"You operated over there."

"Yeah, it was much easier than I figured. I hadn't forgotten much from my surgery. It was like operating in a glare of light. Within my hands." The priest held his fingers up before his face wonderingly. "There were no mistakes. A couple of times I had to do it on the floor of the forest. No one died." Father Elias was silent.

"Did your brother recognize you?"

Elias' voice was very low, "I don't know. He was in a very bad way. It was the first and last time I've been able to do anything at all for him. He's been very close to me since.

"I got the six that tortured him the worst."

"Why bring the hands and feet here to the monastery?"

The cold, superior look the priest turned on him conflicted with the trembling jaw. "They think they're so damn good! Better than everyone else." Venom licked around the edges of the words. "They never say it but . . ." he nodded decisively as if it were an established fact.

The change was abrupt. The anger left his eyes and a little boy look smoothed his features, "I felt at home here, you know, more at home than . . ." a great sigh eased from him, "I've ever felt." In the dim light of the church Father Elias' face was washed as by lightning, the mouth curled again at the right. "They're supposed to know God? Hah! How long would it have taken them to realize what was going on? How long was this God of theirs going to let them live with their blinders?"

"I have a car waiting."

"Yes." Elias got up and accompanied him. After locking the great door of the church behind him, he handed Eli the key.

Eliaphus Daniel Janah watched Walt Bath and John Fay drive off with Father Elias, then walked to the front door of the monastery and rang the bell. When the buzzer opened the door, he entered and went up to the turn. He recognized Sister Damian's Deo gratias.

"Good Morning, Sister." The key was a lead weight in his hand pulling him to the lake bottom. Overburdened, he shifted his stance searching for something to say.

Suddenly, the unbroken maple of the drum started moving slowly to the right, the grain passing before him. He stared into the maw. A wave of infinite compassion spreading from the shadowy interior hit him full in the breast. He drew in a quick, deep breath almost gasping and pulled himself erect.

They stood thus for long silent moments. The tall nun in the grey and brown habit within the cloister. The equally tall detective on the other side by the lobby wall. A smile played over Eli's face. He looked down at the key in the palm of his hand; it was very light after all.

Placing it on the shelf, he gently set the barrel in motion. When he heard Damian lift the metal, he turned and left.

Walking in the heart's wisdom he saw Mir. He was ten paces from the door of the Nissan when the blue Buick came down First and headed toward him up the drive. He stopped abruptly, joy and a sense of foreboding jostling each other within his chest. He stood very still, gravity rooted. The sun rose over the monastery wall and hit him full in the face. A gust of wind whirled a cloud of snow up the slope.

Chapter Seventeen

Merlin must have looked like that before he went down with the Lady of the Lake, his face in the sun, the spirited snow blanketing the lower half of his body. Mir chuckled to herself at her own dreaminess. He had been marvelous. The car parked, she walked up to him and smiled into his eyes. "Leaving?" He nodded. Hesitant, he seemed to be making internal balancing arrangements. Then she realized she hadn't told him about the article. Talk had been entirely unnecessary last night.

She put her hand on his arm, "I'm doing a freelance article on the monastery, that's why I'm here." His eyes widened imperceptibly.

"You?!"

She was piqued. "Yes, me. I'm good you know." She stepped back a little.

He grabbed her hand quickly in both of his. "I didn't mean you weren't good. I meant," his thoughts were racing. He cursed himself for not finding out who was doing the article on the Congregation. "We should talk."

He looked thoughtfully at a snow devil whirling by them

and then back to her. "Did you know we arrested Father Elias this morning?"

The news hit her. So near to home the carnage! That might totally change the direction of the article. She sighed, feeling suddenly very pressured.

"I knew someone was doing a piece." He searched her face. "Did he confess?"

"Yes. You know the way it is," he grimaced, "I can't talk about it yet."

The long end of her scarf whipped behind him and bound them together. His hands felt good. "I . . . I better be going in," she said. "I have an interview with one of the sisters."

He waited until the front door was buzzed open, then got in the car and drove to the office.

He's being extremely cooperative," Eli was watching Fay's fingers tap a drum roll on the file cabinet. "Danley's out of the country. His secretary says he left yesterday for Cambodia."

"Callous about the fix his prelate is in?"

"Unknowing, Elias claims."

"A complete innocent huh?"

"Yep."

"Preposterous."

"The only name he's giving us is O'Reilly. Monsignor Thomas O'Reilly had mercenary ways. No one cares about the purity of his name."

"What about Maysenrod?"

"A man named Robert, he calls 'im, that's all he knew. He flew into Da Nang in '67 and met this guy at the airport. He was outfitted, they picked up half a dozen others, and off they went."

"Janah!" The two of them looked up at the lieutenant's shout. He waved from the door of his office motioning Eli across the floor. Before he took a step from the desk bay where he and John had been talking, he saw the portly figure of the captain in Lieutenant Morley's chair.

"Case closed, Janah, congratulations." He pulled his ponderous bulk up and leaned across the desk. "Good work, Inspector!" Eli felt sordid shaking the flabby, moist palm. The shrewd little eyes in the jowly face watched him. He registered the promotion, but at the same time took in the import of the words that followed. They were connected, too damn connected.

"I read your report. Father Elias' 'Robert' is *not* Bob Maysenrod! I know Bob, great old guy. His brother-in-law is Senator Brimly. Maysenrod's served on more defense committees than any one cares to count. His contacts go all the way up." A bloated finger pointed at the ceiling. "Anyway, who took Father Elias on his supposed tour in 1967 is no concern of ours.

"This business about Elias is going to shake Bishop Danley up," the fleshy cheeks shook sympathetically, "makes his work look bad. He's in Southern Asia right now helping with the arrangements for those orphans—you probably heard about. Shriners offering to do the bone surgery free of charge. He's gotta realize it has no bearing on him at all. There's always a bad apple in the lot." He eyed the silent man before him, "Can't chain your priests down now, can ya?

"Now that this is wrapped up," he looked over at the lieutenant and winked, "we want you to take charge of that high society murder in Bronxville. See Ragusa about it. I've told him I'm handing over the reins; they've gotten nowhere fast."

Strange guy this. He'd just been promoted to full inspector, yet you couldn't read a thing on the guy's face. He could have been talking to a stone Buddah. He waved his hand in dismissal.

So that's the way it's going to be, Eli thought walking back to his desk. He wasn't surprised. He thought of Mir. Then he thought of Danley. No!

There was a sword hanging over him, but it wasn't the slug sitting back there in the lieutenant's chair. Danley played his cards well. It was Mir who was suspended over his head. She would not take meddling in her life lightly. What would be her response if he walked up and said, "Hey, the guy you slept with the other night is an absolute worm."

She was so smart, how the hell could she have let herself in for such a shit load.

No. He couldn't very well confide in her . . . especially after last night. What had been entirely spontaneous and right would look like hard-boiled maneuver.

"Case is closed. I've been promoted to inspector."

Fay's eyes widened. He had never seen such a storm cloud on Eli's face.

I've tried to stay out of this story. But I can't help putting a bean's worth in at this point. My father believed in an orderly, not a haphazard world. Dark followed day. The poles were predictably stable. Sun, moon, stars, planets kept their orbits. We have a universe . . . not chaos.

As above, so below. He believed in law and order.

He was also a Kabbalist and speaking as a Kabbalist, he often remarked that only two levels of his soul were developed. Formation and Creation. Neshama and Ruah. Mother, he said, was strong in the other two. Wisdom and Action. Yichide and Nefesh. This had pulled them together.

When she left him, I think she was trying to develop all four levels. When she left him, he searched and found what was lacking.

He was walking on two legs then and didn't have to be a topologist—a mathematician who deals with the multi-dimensional shape of things—to see the eternal triangle.

Reverend Mother Michaels, wearing a modified version of the habit, groped blindly for a chair and sat down abruptly. "Oh dear Lord, no. No!" She searched Sister Damian's face for a way out. The only thing on Damian's face was the hard, awful truth. Her eyes filled; she began rocking back and forth, tears pouring down her face. She put her hands up to cover her eyes and the hot tears dripped between the fingers. "No . . . no . . . no" Damian knelt down before the older nun, put her arms around the heaving shoulders and held her while she sobbed.

Her pain entered Damian like a frozen knife. It went into her heart and from it liquid freon ran through all her arteries and veins. It couldn't be blood; it was too cold. They rocked together until Mother Michaels' sobs were mute murmurs. A tremendous shudder went through her frame. She sat within the shadow of the other sister's arms completely limp.

They heard six bells off in the distance. Thirty seconds later they heard them again. Only this time they were nearer; the sister ringing for her had come to the head of the stairs. "It's Sister Alice, I asked her to mind the turn." She looked closely at Michaels, "Are you all right?" Mother Michaels nodded weakly. Sister Damian put her hand gently on the other woman's head, then rose and let herself softly out of the narrow cell.

Sister Alice was signing to her that she was expected in the speakroom. She smiled benevolently and signed she would cover the turn. Damian bowed her head thanking her; she had momentarily forgotten the interview.

"Mrs. Janah! Good morning! I'm sorry to keep you waiting." She smiled at Mirari.

"How did you know?"

"What?" The nun leaned forward questioning.

"The name, Janah . . . I was going to tell you."

"Oh . . . no matter. I've known since the first meeting." Her eyes were rimmed in red, but they crinkled up suddenly and little blue darts appeared. "No extra sense," she laughed. "I lost your number. The operator had a Buttrick-Janah listing." She raised her shoulder momentarily, "Your husband was just here."

"Ex-husband."

Sister Damian searched behind the eyes of the woman opposite her. She smiled then, as if humoring a child and repeated it just as before. "Your husband."

Mir suddenly wanted to cry.

She looked into the red-rimmed, gentle eyes for a long moment. "My dear, you better sit down. We have work to do." The voice caused a rill of pleasure. She felt the way she did when she heard the first peeper singing from her wet place in the spring.

"I have been sorting through the archives for what might be helpful to your article." The nun looked at her. There was a weighing in the grey eyes. She pulled her chair up closer to the bars.

"At first," she hesitated. "At first, I was going to select what I thought would look good in print." She looked intently at the bars as if willing them out of her face, or making them a confession. Her head bent into the palm of her hand. It waggled back and forth, "That won't do . . . it will not do! We need to trust you. Father Elias' confession makes many things clear. So many things. You did know about that?" Mir nodded. "Good!"

Sister Damian of Mary sat upright then and said decisively, "I have a proposition. We work together. An hour and a half a day; that is all I can spare. I shouldn't think it would take more than a week. The heavy writing you can do on your own.

"I'll see that a large table is placed out there for your use." She thought a minute, "And a lamp." She noted Mir's silence, "I will not interfere with your actual writing, but I hope you will allow comment.

"I have decided what course of action I should take," she looked away. Mir thought she heard something about a pitfall.

"I have work to do myself, work that I can do here while you are going through all the boxes. I'd be available for questioning. I could help clarify. Do you want to start this morning?"

"Yes."

The tall nun burst from her chair, every part of her habit in motion, "Well, then!" Within ten minutes the door to the cloister opened to the tinkling of a bell and three veiled figures along with Sister Damian pushed a long table through to Mir who caught and pulled it over the threshold. One of the figures, holding her veil out as a tent before her face so that she could see where she was going, reached around a wall and produced a floor lamp. The shade on the old ornate metal lamp came bobbing and dancing forward, the hand holding the black face covering following along behind as far as the door sill.

There was a chittery sound of swallowed laughter from the shortest of the sisters. Her hands full of the boxes of archive material, she stood at the door jamb like a demented sprite. Her veil had caught in her mouth. In between chortles, she was making little puff-puff sounds in an attempt to blow it back out.

Mir, watching the black material fill out below the angle of the nose, deflate and fill again, felt something snap loose within. She burst out laughing. Without hesitation, she reached out and gently pulled the serge from the sister's mouth. Chuckling came from under the veil and the black head bobbed a thank you over the boxes. Mir found herself bobbing in return, still laughing.

Sister Damian's unveiled face behind the other smaller nun smiled at her and nodded as if something had been confirmed. It wasn't blue, Mir thought. The glitter in those grey eyes was the deep purple of amethyst.

After Compline that evening, Sister Damian approached Reverend Mother Michaels, knelt, kissed the floor by her feet, and asked permission to keep an all-night vigil. Mother knew she would be the first to ask. The community who had only learned that Father Allen would be replacing Father Elias and the reason behind this, was still in a state of shock.

Slowly, if she did not watch over them, she would have half the house going without sleep in the chapel. God bless them, some would sleep if a third world war were upon them. She needn't concern herself about them overdoing it.

At 1 a.m. tiny beads of hail hit the windows of the chapel of Annunciation Monastery. They slid on to each other on the cross sections and collected on the sills. The relative heat from the rambling old building, clumped them into random group-ings that would be admired by the postulants in the morning. They would get high on God.

A silent figure, her arms outstretched in the form of a cross, knelt in the darkened church close to the grill, her eyes intent on the tabernacle. A war was going on within Sister Damian.

Words escaped her anguished lips. Something about union and karma was followed by a question of lifetimes and tumul-tuous sobbing. "How many lifetimes? . . ." The question rose in the cold air and reverberated about the nave. The wind threw the bare branches of the trees against the building with increasing frenzy. Distant low grumblings approached and hovered overhead buffeting the old building with sound waves. In the flashes of blinding light that followed, the figure kneeling by the grill looked infinitely weary.

At 5:00 a.m. when the hail quickened to a steady pit-pit, the tall kneeling figure collapsed in a heap on the floor. She was still unconscious when the sister sacristan lit the light on her way to prepare for Mass. She ran to Mother Michaels' cell for help in moving Damian to the infirmary.

Sister Patrick had found Damian flushed and incoherent. "She keeps moaning something about a choice, Reverend Mother. And she's been reciting the Dies Irae over and over again; that's quite clear. At 'Qui Marion absolvisti'—thou, the sinful woman—she becomes hysterical, but somehow contin-ues to the end of the sequence and begins all over again.

"She's very caught up in this Mass of the Dead. Oh, by the way," she looked uncomprehendingly at Michaels, "Bishop Danley's name keeps coming up in the 'Requiem aeternam dona ei domine.'"

Mirari, working alone in the speakroom, became very absorbed in the papers before her.

Monday morning Sister Damian greeted Mirari with a huge grin on her pallid face. There were dark circles under her eyes and the irises were deep purple, not grey.

"I was concerned about you!" Mir gripped the grillwork on her side, watching the nun put a large wicker basket down on the floor by the round table.

Damian looked on her with love. "I'm all right now. A little matter of a decision that had to be made. The vision of living; it got to me," she chuckled low, "but that's universal law. We must make choices. All of time."

Mir was not sure what she was talking about. Was she referring to Father Elias, the choices and decisions he made . . . ? Damian looked deep in her eyes,

"Once we own them, we take them to ourselves," she shuddered as if standing in a strong wind.

Instinctively, Mirari thrust a hand through the grill as far as it would go in a measure of support. The tall sister smiled, "For as many lifetimes . . . however many as it takes to burn up the results."

Sister Damian pulled herself erect. Responding to the look on Mirari's face she spoke to her, "Shush . . . shush . . ." as she would to a baby. "I'm fine, just fine! Now, tell me what you've been doing here. I'm sorry I left you alone yesterday, but maybe it was just as well. You had a chance for an overall look in peace and quiet. Some beginning intuitions about how you'll handle it."

As she pored through the materials Damian had put at her

disposal, Mirari Buttrick Janah had been sitting on a growing excitement. A sizable picture of power and greed was taking shape.

She had never been convinced that an orderly sequence was appropriate in writing. Something more like a spiral felt right. Sidling up to the facts, then floating away, was much more satisfactory than hitting them on the head with a baseball bat. There was intelligence out there. Let them draw their own conclusions. It was more of a dance than a boardroom report.

Last night looking over her notes by the fireplace, her thoughts kept going back to Danley's secret cache. Surrounded by visions of these munitions, some of her notes acquired a sinister character.

The more she saw, the less she understood his permission to write the article. Was he so secure? Did he think the bedclothes tossing they engaged in was going to hog-tie and bind her? Didn't he care? She felt the power of the man again. What had he wanted? Did anyone really know what she wanted or were they all just opportunists taking what they could as it came along? So many questions.

She looked across at Sister Damian working steadily at her sewing. "You know, Sister, this is not the article I thought I would be writing."

"It never is, Mirari." The eyes shone. "We were so caught up in what we were doing, I'm afraid we did not notice the inconsistencies." She took a deep breath.

She resumed her work. She was pulling fine threads from the lining of a dark green cope.

"That's a beautiful vestment!"

"Yes. We have put a lot of work into it. It's a Christmas gift." With great care and concentration she separated the remaining fibers. She must have had some preordained plan in mind for she began sewing little blocks like Morse code fragments together in bundles.

"Who is going to see the lining?" Mir was entranced at the care the nun was taking.

"The one who matters," came the tongue in cheek reply.

"Words are very powerful beings Mirari," Sister Damian's voice lowered, "a malediction, fully consented, backed by free will . . . well, it is probably better that most do not know, at this time, what can be built up . . . what can be pulled down."

Three people in Westchester County were extremely conscious of Bishop Danley's arrival at Kennedy International the following Sunday.

Eli buried himself in the new investigation, grateful for Bath and Fay's unspoken support. He otherwise resumed a monk's existence. He left a message with Marion's answering service saying he would be extremely busy. Although he wanted to very much, he did not contact Mir.

Every particle of him wanted to face Danley but his own energy was so riled, so out of touch with the Chi, that he could not in all sanity trust it. Little more than a brute urge to break the guy's neck, it was, and where would that lead? He watched the press conference Danley had called for that evening.

Mir also watched Danley on TV. She watched his deferential handling of the reporters. His work in Southeast Asia for the orphans? Totally insignificant beside the enormous amount that others had done. He did little more than arrange passage.

But the reporters really wanted to know about Elias. Is it possible he had no previous knowledge? "No previous knowledge . . . not a clue." His voice became sonorous . ;. . "There is forgiveness in the house of the Lord for the worst sinner . . ."

Mir watching, knew she had to see him face to face. There was something she had to know. She called his unlisted number.

He was brusque, "Why don't you come down tonight? The hoopla's died down."

"It's too late . . . the last train left."

His voice was deliberate, "I'll send the car."

Sister Damian worked on the brilliant green vestments long after the community was asleep. The words she painstakingly inserted would be seen by no one, that is, unless they opened the lining and held it to the light. Each word was built from threads removed. In minute, invisible lightstitch Damian lay the Dies Irae down. There was no room for mistake.

For a moment, riding the cage elevator, Mir was frightened. Why had she come? To see his face when she told him what she knew? To know why? A cold shiver went down her spine. She looked down grimly at the floor of the elevator. Her jaw set then, and she placed both feet squarely on the snake's head.

She didn't kick off her shoes this time. "We need to talk." He smiled and took her coat, but there was a crafty glint in his eyes. He weighed the woman, the set of her shoulders, the stance.

"Coffee?"

"Yes." She followed him into the kitchen.

"How was the ride down?"

"Comfortable. The roads were slick, but we had no trouble."

"That car's a beaut!" he said with pride.

She blurted it. She was never good at holding back. Her voice, soft and powerful with an undercurrent of steel, drove the words into his turned back. "I see a callous indifference to human life. The man I thought I saw does not exist. Manipulation, abuse of power . . . I'm at a loss. Do you want more?"

"No." He turned and gave her a level look. "That's the way it is, huh?" Mir tried to read his eyes, but a bland indifference had been dropped. "I thought we were alike, you and I." He turned back to lift the finished coffee and pour it into the heavy glasses, "Guess I was wrong."

Mir was dumbfounded. "You thought I would go along with the activities of the past twenty–thirty years?" She could not believe her ears. She took a mouthful of the hot coffee. "I'm going to report on every one of them."

"Too bad!" The malevolence was real now, the powerful features had shed every aspect of amiability, the mouth was cruel and sneering. "I wouldn't." He walked over and stood above her. "Since that's the way the wind blows, I'll help myself to what I want tonight."

A bruised and battered Mirari Buttrick Janah was delivered by black Lincoln to the back door of her home just before dawn. She called in sick at the office. Then she called the monastery and left a message for Sister Damian; she would need a couple of days, she had come down with the flu. She slept.

Christmas Eve Mass in the Cathedral that year was extremely beautiful. Three officiating bishops clad in the green vestments of hope called for hope in the coming of the Spirit. Hundreds of candles sent their flickering lights out into the hearts of the accumulated faithful.

The scent of fresh flowers filled the church. Sculptured red pointsetta daggers punctuated the white arrangements on either side of the high altar.

Newspaper articles later hinted that Bishop Danley had contracted some obscure viral infection on his recent trip to Asia. One young seminarian, helping him to robe up before the ceremonies, thought he began acting strange as soon as he slipped the exquisite new chasuble over his head.

Everybody was perspiring. With all the candles that were burning, the sanctuary was like a mini inferno.

No one could quite believe that he was dead. With an anguished cry, he keeled over at the joint consecration. The seminarians acting as altar boys ran first for the host he dropped. With great care, they held the circle of bread until it was decided that they should consume it. Figuring he had fainted, they did not rush as quickly to Danley's side.

Mirari Buttrick Janah finished a very well documented article. It won her prizes.

She asked Eliaphus Daniel Janah to move back into the house two years afterwards. Merely a formality. He had been living there most of the time.

Sister Damian of Mary was elected to a six-year term as Mother Superior when Mother Michaels' term expired. She made some interesting changes in the order's function, changes that attracted many women to their life.

Father Elias served a two-year prison term. Upon release, shorn of his priestly duties, he found a job as a carpenter.

* * *